BEYOND EARTH

THE COLLECTED TALES, VOLUME 1: NEW EARTH

Dr S. Fern

Published by New Generation Publishing in 2016

Copyright © Dr S. Fern 2016

First Edition

The author asserts the moral right under the Copyright, Designs and Patents Act 1988 to be identified as the author of this work.

All Rights reserved. No part of this publication may be reproduced, stored in a retrieval system or transmitted, in any form or by any means without the prior consent of the author, nor be otherwise circulated in any form of binding or cover other than that which it is published and without a similar condition being imposed on the subsequent purchaser.

Cover image sourced from www.pixabay.com and is free of copyrights under Creative Commons CCO.

www.newgeneration-publishing.com

ACKNOWLEDGEMENTS

I would like to thank Sean 'the AD caveman' Young for his continued help and support.

Contents

The Alabama State Incident 1

Seeds of Terror 33

Exodus 47

Old Lies 81

The Orphans Return 95

Vanguard 111

Post-human 131

Temporal Invariance 159

Picaroon 175

Return to the Anderson System 195

THE ALABAMA STATE INCIDENT

The Peerless was a mining dreadnought operating out of CR12, an ore processing plant in orbit around New Jupiter, the fourth planet of the New Earth system. She was one of three vessels mining the proto-moons that orbited the gas giant.

'We're about to enter disputed space, Captain,' Navigation Officer Higgins reported, a note of concern in his voice.

'Very good, Higgins. Order all stop and maintain station keeping,' Captain Roberts responded without looking up from his command console. Its numerous screens presented him with details of every one of the ship's systems. Holding a finger to his earpiece, the captain spoke into a small microphone that extended round to his mouth. 'Mr Holt, report to the bridge.' The order rang across the ship's intercom.

Two minutes later Shaun Holt, the ship's chief geologist entered the bridge and presented himself to the captain. 'You sent for me, Captain?'

'Yes, thank you. I'd like you to take a look at the survey results for the moon we're due to mine. I want to know if it's valuable enough to upset the Coalition over.'

Holt sat down at workstation seven, entered his login credentials, and began to analyse the results of the morning's survey.

'It looks like it is, Captain.'

'Right. Higgins, are there any Coalition vessels in the area?'

'No, Captain, not at the moment.'

'Good, take us in to low orbit. Mr Wolf, order the drills prepared.'

'At once, Captain… but what if a patrol catches us whilst we're drilling?' Mr Wolf, the chief operations officer, asked. 'I've heard they've fired on vessels they find operating within their space.'

'We are not in *their space*, Mr Wolf; this is disputed space. The fact that it's claimed by both the Federated American States and the South American Coalition means that no one can claim sovereignty over these moons – you know this as well as I do. Now, stop panicking and prepare the drills.'

'Aye aye, Sir.' The chief's concerns were well founded; it was well known that the S.A.C. policed their space aggressively. In the first few decades after the initial colonisation of New Earth, the various nations, alliances and coalitions had raced to lay claim to as much of the new system's resources as possible. The inner planets, along with their moons, had been claimed first, but the outer planets required a much greater outlay of resources to claim with any surety. Here, in the outer reaches of the system, clear, defined borders didn't exist – disputes were common place.

Within half an hour, however, Mr Wolf had sent the Peerless' six enormous drills towards the surface of the moon. The drills were attached to large umbilical cords which served not only to supply them with power and provide a means of communication with the mother-ship, but also allowed the mined rock to be transported directly to the Peerless' holds. In this way the dreadnought was able to extract mineral-rich rock without having to set up manned operations on the moon's surface.

***

The Peerless had been in orbit, mining the moon's mineral-rich rock, for just under a week when the contact alarm sounded on the navigation officer's console.

'Chief, I'm reading a vessel approaching from starboard,' the assistant navigator announced, breaking the silence that had settled on the bridge.

'Identification?' the Peerless' chief mate enquired.

'She's broadcasting an S.A.C. call sign… the S.A.C. Tambio – a class 46 frigate. She'll be here in about five minutes.'

'Five minutes? Why didn't we detect her sooner?'

'We're in low orbit, Chief; she's only just come over the horizon.'

'Damn,' the chief cursed as he activated the comm-link set into his chair.

'Yes, what is it?' The captain sounded groggy.

'I'm sorry to wake you, Captain; it's Chief Roberts – we've just detected an S.A.C. frigate on an intercept course; she'll be here in five minutes. I thought you should know.'

'Five minutes? All right, I'm on my way.'

A couple of minutes later the captain jogged onto the bridge, his boots unlaced and his shirt unbuttoned. 'How long until—'

'She's entering range now, Captain.'

'On screen.'

***

The Tambio was one of the South American Coalition's advanced laser frigates; she was fast and her silhouette slight. With a pair of dorsal-mounted turrets forward of her superstructure and another pair aft, each mounting a single high powered laser, she was reasonably well armed for a vessel of her displacement. She also boasted a fearsome array of torpedo launchers amidships as well as ventrally-mounted void mine layers.

The Tambio's commander, Frigate-captain Carolina Martinez was a young woman in her early thirties. She had a tanned complexion and long walnut-brown hair that she kept pinned in a bun at the base of her neck.

After adjusting her slightly peaked cap she addressed the mining ship. 'Peerless, this is Frigate-captain Martinez of the S.A.C. navy. You are mining in space that is sovereign to the South American Coalition. You will cease your operations immediately.'

'S.A.C. Tambio, this is Captain Roberts of the Peerless, this region is currently disputed – no one has sovereignty. Your accusation is groundless. Stand down.'

'Captain Roberts, you will stop drilling immediately or I will be forced to take action,' Captain Martinez snapped before turning to her navigation officer. 'Lieutenant Silva, plot a course and take us within range. Lieutenant Morales, cycle the lasers up to full power and target their drills.'

'Aye, Captain,' the two officers replied in unison.

On board, the Peerless Navigation officer Higgins watched as the Tambio began her approach.

'Captain, they're targeting the drills!'

'Mr Wolf, get them up NOW!'

'It'll take a couple of minutes to shut them down, Captain, never mind retract the umbilical cords.'

'I don't care how you do it, just get it done!' the captain snapped as he watched the Tambio's turrets lock on to the drills.

'I am ready to open fire, Frigate-captain,' Lieutenant Morales said.

'Good. Open fire, Lieutenant.'

Captain Roberts watched in impotent rage as the Tambio's lasers fired salvo after salvo into the dreadnought's drills. Explosions lit up the void, but the fires that would usually follow guttered and died in the vacuum. Before long the drills were little more than piles of molten slag, the severed umbilical cords sparked, but otherwise hung dead in space.

'I'm sorry, Captain, the drills are gone,' Mr Wolf reported quietly.

The captain was silent as he watched the Tambio turn to starboard and continue on her patrol.

'Return us to the processing plant,' he growled as he stalked off the bridge.

***

Capable of docking several hundred vessels simultaneously, Archangel Spaceport was visible at night from the surface of New Earth. Jointly run by the European Union and the Federated American States, the colossal space station was larger even than Novorinya Station – the Russian naval base that orbited much further from the planet.

'Wilkins, please send for Captain Price.' Admiral Pierce lifted his finger from the intercom and cut the link with his aide in the next room. This news from the Peerless was bad, very bad the admiral reflected, as he lit a large cigar and stood by his window that looked out over the docks and into the void beyond. The S.A.C. were becoming more assertive over their claims to the disputed outer-system regions. The Federated States could ill afford to officially enter another conflict. Even with the European Union on side, the constant border disputes with the Pan Asian Alliance were a major drain on resources and manpower. That said, New Jupiter's resource-rich moons and the CR12 processing plant were vital assets that had to be protected. The South American Coalition would need to be reminded that they could not act against the Federation with impunity.

A knock at the dark wood door broke the admiral's train of thoughts.

'Come in,' he said as he turned and walked back towards his desk.

'Captain Price, Admiral,' his aid announced from the other room as an older uniformed man entered.

'Ah, Captain Price, please, take a seat,' the admiral said as the captain crossed the office and shook his proffered hand.

'Thank you, Admiral,' the old captain replied in a gruff voice that spoke either of many years bellowing orders or heavy smoking, but probably both.

'Cigar?' the admiral asked, sliding a wooden box across the table.

'Thank you.' The captain took one of the admirals' cigars, bit off the end and held it between yellowed teeth to light it.

'It's bad news I'm afraid, Richard.'

'What have the damned 'Alliance' done now?'

'It's not the 'Alliance' this time. The S.A.C. are rattling the sabre over New Jupiter again. One of our mining dreadnoughts has been attacked.'

'How badly?'

'They just destroyed her drills. No one was hurt, but that is not the point.'

'Not the point at all, Sir; if they've grown bold enough to start openly attacking foreign shipping then it's just a matter of time before things escalate.'

'Quite so. That is why I want you to take the Alabama State out to New Jupiter and ensure that something like this doesn't happen again; you'll be making a statement.'

'Quite a statement indeed, Sir. If I may ask, why the Alabama State?'

'She's just completed her refit – she's the most advanced battleship in the fleet. Besides, she's the only capital ship not currently patrolling The Field or tied up with the Europeans against the Asians,' the admiral concluded.

***

The F.S.S. Alabama State was an impressive ship. She was one of the largest vessels in the Federated States' fleet. Previously armed with batteries of laser cannons, she had recently been re-fitted. All of her dorsal and ventral turrets had been re-armed with United Industries' newly developed heavy ion cannons. Though they could not boast the range of the laser batteries they replaced, they were far more powerful. Her secondary armament had remained unchanged. Set along her flanks she boasted ten individually mounted heavy lasers; five to port and five to starboard. When these armaments were considered alongside her formidable close-in defensive systems, it became obvious that the admiralty's boast that she was nigh-on unassailable was not a hollow one.

It would take the best part of two weeks to reach New Jupiter; two weeks that Captain Price intended to use to ensure that his crew were well acquainted with their ship's new systems.

On their arrival at the CR12 processing plant, Captain Price was introduced to Captain Roberts of the Peerless.

'Pleased to meet you, Captain,' Captain Roberts said as he shook hands with the old captain.

'Likewise, Captain,' Price replied through a haze of cigar smoke. 'You've been having some trouble with the Coalition I hear?'

'Some trouble?' Roberts replied. 'Let me show you something, Captain.' Roberts led the old man to a viewing platform above the huge docks. Passing Price a pair of magnoculars, he motioned the captain towards quay three where the Peerless was docked. As they watched, what appeared to be a huge ring of scrap metal was being lifted out of one of the Peerless' holds.

'Do you see that, Captain?' Roberts asked. 'That is all that remains of one of my drills; a mounting ring, and not much of a ring at that. *That* is my trouble, Captain. Each of those drills were worth a small fortune and they destroyed all six of them, all six!'

After considering the ruined piece of machinery for a minute Captain Price turned to the Peerless' captain. 'You know exactly who did this, do you, Captain?'

'I do, Captain Price, I do,' Roberts growled. 'The S.A.C. Tambio.'

'I see…' Price trailed off in thought. 'What class is the Tambio?'

'I'm not sure, Captain; I'm the commander of a dreadnought, not a warship. She was fast and armed – we were neither," Roberts stated defensively.

'I didn't mean to criticise you, Captain; your ship is still space-worthy and your crew were not injured. You did as much as could be expected in the circumstances.'

'What would you have done, Captain?' Roberts asked as the two men turned and left the quayside.

'What would I have done? I command a battleship, Captain; the situation would have been very different. No, we will not dwell on what is passed, instead we will discuss what must be done to ensure that Federated States' registered vessels can carry out their business unmolested,' he concluded with a wide grin that was punctuated by a glowing cigar stub.

It took a further five days for the six replacement drills to be fitted to the Peerless. As soon as they had been fitted and tested the Peerless put to space, accompanied by Captain Price and the Alabama State. Together they headed back to the proto-moon where he had encountered the Tambio.

***

The Peerless was preparing to lower her drills when the Tambio sailed into view once again, this time training her lasers on the Peerless herself, rather than her drills.

'Continue as you are, Captain; leave this to me.' Captain Price's confident voice filled the Peerless' bridge, reassuring the dreadnought's crew.

'You heard the captain; Mr Wolf, lower the drills,' Roberts snapped.

'Aye aye, Sir.'

As the Peerless was lowering her drills the F.S.S. Alabama State placed herself directly between the mining ship and the approaching S.A.C. frigate.

'Do not target the Tambio,' Captain Price ordered. 'Not until I give the order.'

'This is Frigate-captain Martinez of the S.A.C. Tambio. You are once again drilling in sovereign S.A.C. territory. You will stop immediately. You will not be given a second chance.'

'This is Captain Price of the *battleship* F.S.S. Alabama State neither my vessel nor the Peerless are within S.A.C. territory; this is a disputed region – you have no authority here. Go home, Frigate-captain.'

'Captain, they've loaded their torpedo tubes,' the ensign reported. 'I don't understand…'

'They are trying to cow us into submission, Ensign: Captain Martinez knows that if we attack her ship, the S.A.C. will take it as a declaration of war,' Commander Morris explained from the far side of the bridge.

'I like her,' Captain Price commented.

'Captain?'

'I have respect for her, that is all, Commander. Target the Tambio – two can play her game.'

'Lock the heavy lasers onto the Tambio.'

'No, Commander, charge the ion cannons – we are here to make a statement, so let's make one.'

'Aye aye, Sir. Charge main weapons.'

'Frigate-captain Martinez, this is Captain Price; your torpedoes will cause little more than superficial damage, assuming they make contact at all. I can and will vaporise your ship if I am forced to, believe me.'

The Tambio did not back down.

'Commander, fire a warning show across her bow.

'Aye aye, Sir.' Commander Morris turned to the battleship's primary fire control officer. 'Lieutenant-commander Hunter, prepare to put a shot across her bow.'

'Aye aye, Sir.'

The magnetic accelerators of the forward dorsal turret glowed blue-white as the weapon charged.

'Fire!'

A sudden blinding light flashed from the cannon's barrel as it spat a bolt of white-hot plasma towards the S.A.C. frigate. The bow of the Tambio erupted into a ball of flame a split second after the ship's dispersion field collapsed.

'WHAT HAPPENED?!' Commander Morris roared. 'I told you to put a shot *across* her bow, not *into* it!'

'I'm sorry, Commander, I guess the targeting computer was a little out...' the lieutenant-commander spluttered.

'I suggest you *completely* recalibrate the targeting system, Lieutenant-commander,' Captain Price said quietly as he watched the Tambio roll over to port and limp away.

***

Frigate-captain Martinez's gaze was fixed on the main view screen, on the imposing form of the F.S.S. Alabama State. She stood statuesque, leaning on the rail that enclosed the command deck, her dark brown hair tied up in a tight bun, her uniform clean and crisp.

'Captain, I'm detecting an energy build up in their forward dorsal turret.'

'Remain calm, Ensign, they won't open fire – they can't afford to, not out here,' she replied in a venomous tone. She didn't take her eyes from the view screen. 'They'll back down – they won't risk war over a moon.'

The frigate-captain's stony countenance was shattered a second later when the battleship opened fire. Shock froze her in place as the shot crossed the void. That shock, along with the tense silence on the bridge, was banished when the shot impacted, the dispersion field collapsed, and the frigate's bow was engulfed in white-hot plasma. The bridge was battered by secondary explosions. Martinez was thrown from the command deck into a stanchion and blacked out.

When she came to the bridge was in chaos: fires were burning out of control; there had been several structural collapses; all the lights had failed and the air filtration system was failing to filter out the smoke that was threatening to fill the bridge. She was in pain and couldn't move her right arm.

'Captain, this is Lieutenant Alonso, can you hear me?' the ship's doctor asked through a respirator.

'Yes,' she rasped, coughing painfully as she breathed in a lungful of smoke. 'I can hear you, lieutenant. What's the status of the ship?'

'We've taken heavy damage to the bow, everything forward of the bridge has been completely destroyed. I need to get you off the bridge, Captain; the fires are out of control. Can you move?'

'Yes,' she replied and struggled through the pain to her feet. The bridge jolted as another explosion below decks rocked the stricken ship. The captain reached out instinctively to steady herself with her right arm but missed the ruined terminal she had been reaching for. She looked down and noticed for the first time that her right arm stopped just below the elbow. Lieutenant Alonso caught her as she passed out for the second time.

The next time she woke the she was in the sick bay.

'The captain's awake, Doctor.'

'Thank you, Nadia,' Lieutenant Alonso replied. 'Ah, Captain, how do you feel?'

'My right side hurts and I've got a splitting headache, but other than that, not too bad, considering,' she replied, her voice groggy. It took a few minutes for her to remember what had happened. Initially she could only recall a series of explosions, a flying sensation, pain and then nothing. Slowly, however, her memories returned and she looked down at her arm.

'I'm sorry about your arm, Captain, I really am but I didn't have a choice; it was trapped underneath a collapsed bulkhead – I had to amputate it in order to save you.' The young doctor sounded distraught. The captain felt numb; she didn't know quite what to think. Instead she asked, 'Is Lieutenant Moreno still alive?'

'Yes, Captain; he was injured, but not badly. He is currently commanding the ship from the engine room.'

'I would like to see him, Lieutenant.'

'Of course, I'll have him sent up; you must continue to rest.'

'Very well.'

Several minutes later Lieutenant Moreno arrived at the sick bay. 'Captain, it's so good to see you awake.'

'Thank you, Lieutenant; it's good to be awake. What's our status?'

The lieutenant grimaced. 'Our bow has been completely destroyed – there's nothing left of the ship fore of the bridge, and that's inoperable. We've taken serious damage amidships and the field capacitors are all blown, but the rear turrets are still operational and the main drive is undamaged.'

'Can we make Port Vercuro?'

'Yes, Captain, I've set a course, but we can only cruise at half speed. We've taken too much damage to risk anything more, especially without the protection of a field.'

The captain cursed, then immediately regretted it as her headache made its presence known. 'Just get us back to port, Lieutenant,' she said before collapsing back onto the bed.

***

It took the Tambio several weeks to limp back to Port Vercuro – the mid-system S.A.C. naval base situated between the orbits of New Jupiter and the third planet of the New Earth system, Perun – a journey that would normally only take a week. By the time she arrived, however, Frigate-captain Martinez was back on her feet.

As she disembarked she was met by a junior officer. 'Frigate-captain Martinez? I am Second-lieutenant Santos; Vice-admiral Vasquez's aide. Could you come with me, please?'

'The vice-admiral wants to de-brief me so soon? Very well, lead on.'

The vice-admiral's office was comfortable and well furnished. Pictures of famous Coalition ships lined the walls, the lighting was warm and the leather chairs either side of the large desk were well padded.

'Ah, Frigate-captain Martinez, please, come in,' Vice-admiral Vasquez said as she was ushered into the room. 'Please, take a seat. I hear you have had a run in with the Federated States' navy? I would appreciate it if you could bring me up to speed. This isn't a formal de-briefing – I'm aware that you are probably very tired and in need of rest – the official de-briefing can wait until tomorrow.'

'We were patrolling the outer moons of New Jupiter when we encountered a mining dreadnought in orbit above a proto-moon,' she began.

'Another Carter Resources vessel?'

'The same one – the Peerless. This time she was escorted by a battleship, the F.S.S. Alabama State. I confronted them and told them that they were, once again, violating our territory. That is when I was fired upon.'

'By the Alabama State?'

'Yes, Vice-admiral, their salvo wrecked the bridge and completely destroyed everything forward of it. It was a miracle we made it back at all, Sir.' The frigate-captain's voice was stony and laced with bitterness.

'A miracle? Yes, that's a fair way of putting it. You and your crew are to be commended, Frigate-captain.'

'You mean those who made it back. Just over half of the Tambio's crew are dead, Vice-admiral. It's always the same. How many more good people are going to die at the hands of the Federated States?' she snapped.

'I understand your frustration, Frigate-captain; you have a brother in the navy, don't you?'

'Not anymore; he was killed serving on the Intrépida.'

'I'm sorry for your loss, truly, I am. This is why we must continue to resist foreign aggression – those who have given their lives in service to the Coalition, their deaths must count for something.'

'We *are* going to strike back, aren't we, Vice-admiral?'

'You can be sure of it; I will bring this to Admiral Fernández's attention immediately. In the meantime I want you to report to the surgeon-general and have that arm looked at – I'll not have officers under my command anything less than 100% fit for duty.'

'Aye aye, Sir.'

'Dismissed, Frigate-captain.' As she turned to leave the vice-admiral activated the intercom. 'Santos, send Mr Silva to see me as soon as possible.'

***

The assault craft floated through the void undetected. With all of its major systems powered down, the weak signal of its life-support system was barely detectable. The ten man commando squad on board had been in semi-hibernation ever since their small craft had been launched from an escort carrier on silent running, just over thirty-six hours previously.

It was a high-risk operation; if they missed their target they would end up dying a long, lingering death drifting endlessly through the void. Fortunately the F.S.S. Alabama State had not made any sudden course corrections and the assault craft drifted slowly and silently through the battleship's starboard dispersion field. Designed to stop high energy, high velocity objects, the field was powerless to prevent a slow object drifting through.

A dull *thud* indicated successful contact with the battleship. The docking ring secured itself with a soft *shuck*. A green light blinked on, the assault craft powered up and its systems came back on-line. As the life-support system was resuscitating the commandos, automated plasma burners began cutting through the battleship's colossal armour plating. As soon as the last of the hull plating had turned to molten slag and slewed to the deck the commandos dived through the white-hot opening and into what appeared to be a service corridor.

After glancing at a forearm-mounted data slate the leader of the commando team chopped the air and began leading the team along the corridor in the direction of the bridge. The team's infiltration had been a complete success; they met no resistance as they jogged along the corridor and entered a service duct. After climbing and crawling for several minutes the team halted at hatch marked 'B07'. One of the commandos released the locking mechanism and swung the hatch open. A second later the team leader dived out onto the bridge, rolled away from the hatchway and came up firing. The rest of the team followed and in a few seconds the bridge was a hell of laser carbine fire.

***

'Captain, I'm picking up some strange readings from the Alabama State,' the Peerless' assistant navigator reported.

'What is it, Mr Young?' Captain Roberts asked.

'They've just stopped broadcasting their F.S. call sign, Captain.'

'That's odd…'

'No, Sir, it's worrying – look.'

The captain crossed the bridge to the navigator's console. 'That's an S.A.C. call sign. Bring her up on the main view screen.' A chill went through Captain Roberts as he tried to make sense of the cloud that was surrounding the battleship. 'I want a high-resolution scan now, Mr Young. I want you to tell me it's just vented plasma that's surrounding her.'

'I… Oh Hell, Captain, that's not plasma, it's the crew – look.' Mr Young magnified the view until a section of her starboard side filled the screen. 'It looks like the entire ship has been—'

'Voided…'

'But how? Surely there are safeguards in place to prevent something like that?'

'There are: this wasn't an accident.'

'How can you be sure?' another of the bridge crew asked.

'The change in call sign for one thing, and for another, that there – magnify the top right hand corner of the screen.' As the view was magnified a small assault craft came into focus.

'How in Hell's name could it have got through the field *and* the point defences?'

'Silent running perhaps; I don't know. What I do know is that we need to get out of here right now. Raise the drills and send out a priority message to CR12 *and* Archangel.'

***

The light cruiser S.A.C. Valiente came to a halt a few hundred kilometres off the Alabama State's starboard quarter and launched a skiff from her launch bay. Several minutes later the small craft docked with the drifting battleship and a tall, slim man disembarked. He was clean-shaven and wore a long dark coat with a high collar. He was followed by the newly promoted Captain Martinez and half a dozen other S.A.C. officers. They were met by eight of the commandos.

'I am Mr Silva – naval intelligence. You must be Unit Six,' he said. 'You've done well. You are to return to Port Vercuro; Captain Martinez will take command of the Alabama State.' Turning to the young captain, he continued in a dark tone he did not attempt to conceal. 'Congratulations on your new command, Captain.' He then turned and re-embarked the skiff. 'Unit Six, follow me; the Valiente will return you to port.'

***

Admiral Pierce had just shaken hands with the latest officer to enter his office, a portly vice-admiral with thinning brown hair, when his intercom activated. 'Admiral, Miss Harris has just arrived.'

'Send her in, Wilkins,' the admiral replied before cutting the link to his aide. A few seconds later a woman in her mid-thirties entered the room. Her slate grey suit set her apart from the gathered naval officers; other than an identity card that displayed her level 7 security clearance, she wore no identifying insignia at all.

'Ah, Miss Harris, good morning. May I introduce Vice-admiral Adams, Colonel Baker—'

'Commander of the Void Assault Brigade,' Miss Harris interrupted the Admiral. 'And this is Doctor Allen from the Advanced Weapons Research Institute. Thank you, Admiral – I think we can dispense with the pleasantries.'

'*You* might know who *we* are, Miss Harris, but I don't think I'm the only one here who is at a loss as to who *you* are,' the old grizzled colonel growled.

'Colonel, please. Gentlemen, this is Miss Harris from Department 12.'

'Foreign Intelligence?' Doctor Allen asked.

'Yes. Shall we begin?' the admiral replied as he took his seat on the far side of his large desk. The others each took a seat in silence. 'I've called you here today because we've lost contact with one of our ships.'

'Which one?' Adams asked.

'The Alabama State. She was escorting a Carter Resources mining dreadnought that was operating out of CR12.'

'CR12?' the doctor asked.

'An ore processing plant in orbit around New Jupiter,' the admiral explained.

'Do we know why we've lost contact?' Adams asked.

'There is strong possibility that—'

'The S.A.C. have seized the Alabama State. She's currently docked at Port Vercuro,' the intelligence agent said, again interrupting the admiral.

'You can't be serious? The Coalition has a history of harassing foreign vessels around New Jupiter but it's never attacked one before,' the vice-admiral cut in.

'It has now – the evidence is clear,' Harris replied.

'How did you—'

'I work for Department 12; it's my job to know these things, Admiral.'

'Well for the benefit of those of us who still have no idea *precisely* what's going on, do you think we might take a look at this evidence?' the colonel snapped.

'Admiral, with your permission?' Harris took a small data stick out of her inside breast pocket and stood up.

'Certainly,' the admiral replied, rising from his chair.

Harris walked around the desk, sat down in the admiral's seat and inserted the data stick into the desk-mounted console. 'Six weeks ago a Carter Resources dreadnought, the Peerless, in orbit around a proto-moon of New Jupiter, was attacked by the S.A.C. Tambio – a class 46 frigate. Her drills were destroyed. In response, the admiral dispatched the F.S.S. Alabama State to New Jupiter.'

'We needed to show that weren't going to be cowed by the Coalition's aggression,' the admiral interjected.

'Quite right,' Colonel Baker agreed.

'Suffice to say that the Peerless, escorted by the Alabama State, returned to the proto-moon and continued mining.'

'Whereupon they were attacked by the Tambio?'

'Not quite, Colonel. Whereupon the Alabama State opened fire and nearly destroyed the Tambio.'

'Without provocation?'

'We don't know why she opened fire,' the admiral said, just as Harris was about to speak. 'It's possible that she was forced to – we just don't know.'

'That much is true – we don't know *why* she fired on the Tambio, but we do know that the S.A.C. responded. This is a recording of the Alabama State, made by the Peerless, shortly before she returned to CR12.'

The three men leaned over the desk as the inset screen displayed a view of the void with the Alabama State at its centre.

'This is a view of the battleship just after it stopped broadcasting its F.S. call sign.'

'What's that haze surrounding the ship?' Doctor Allen asked.

'That's not a haze, Doctor. In a second the Peerless' captain orders the view magnified.' Sure enough the image of the Alabama State was magnified a couple of seconds later until the bodies floating around the ship came into focus. The colonel and the doctor both took sharp breaths.

'How?'

'The answer to that, colonel, will become clear in a minute… there,' Harris replied as the view shifted to focus on the assault craft attached to the battleship's hull. 'I have had this image clarified – it's clearly an S.A.C. assault craft.'

The recording froze and Harris called up a shot of the assault craft that had been cleaned up. Colonel Baker studied the image for several minutes.

'You're right, it's definitely a Tiburon class assault craft. They're short ranged so there must have been a carrier in the vicinity.'

'Never mind that, how the bloody hell did it get past the Alabama's field and point defences?' Vice-admiral Adams snapped.

'We… don't know,' Harris mumbled.

'If the craft were travelling slowly enough a dispersion field wouldn't stop it,' the colonel said.

'But the point defences should have destroyed it before it got that close, Colonel,' the vice-admiral countered.

'If they'd powered down everything except life-support it's possible the sensors wouldn't detect it.'

'What you're suggesting, colonel is—'

'Extremely high-risk and unlikely to succeed, I know, Miss Harris. We tried developing similar tactics in the 'Brigade` but concluded that the risk of failure was too high.'

'Well it seems to have worked here. A single unit managed to board the Alabama State, storm the bridge and void the rest of the ship.'

'The question is, what are we going to do about it?' Admiral Pierce interrupted. 'Doctor, have you got anything to contribute?'

'Erm, well, the new class of void armour that's almost ready to be field-tested should provide the colonel's men with many advantages over their current equipment.'

'My marines would still need to board the ship, Doctor. You can be sure that the S.A.C. are currently upgrading the ship's point defence sensor arrays to prevent us taking her back in the same way we lost her.

'Okay, well, we're also working with phased plasma – it should boost the output of our ion cannons by about twenty per cent.'

'We don't want to destroy the Alabama State, Doctor, we want to re-take her. Does anything *else* come to mind?' The admiral's patience was clearly running out.

'I, er, I don't think so, no. I'm sorry, Admiral.'

The admiral was about to reply when Harris interrupted him again. 'Admiral, I'm aware of some work currently being done planet-side by United Industries.'

'Just what kind of work, Miss Harris?'

'A new infiltration asset, Admiral. I think it might be the answer you're looking for.'

'Go on.'

'They've completed the major developmental work and are about to begin field tests. I'm sure they could be convinced that our current situation would provide them with a perfect test environment.'

'How did you find out about this? U.I. are fastidious about security to the point of fanaticism.'

'I'm afraid that's classified, Colonel,' she replied. 'I suggest that you contact Doctor Milsen, the technical director, and explain the situation. I suspect he will offer to recover the Alabama State in return for an opportunity to field-test the new asset. We shouldn't have to reveal to them how much we know.'

'You mean we shouldn't have to reveal how much *you* know,' the colonel sneered.

'You may not have much respect for me or my work, Colonel, but I assure you, my department and I are invaluable. You would do well to remember that.' Harris' tone became dangerous.

'That's enough, both of you,' Pierce snapped. 'I think we've achieved all we can. Thank you all for your time, you are dismissed.'

The admiral let out a long, tired breath once he was alone. He needed to recover the Alabama State, but couldn't afford to risk war with the Coalition. He was walking on thin ice and it would only get thinner the moment he contacted United Industries.

***

Harris was right: Doctor Milsen invited the admiral along with Vice-admiral Adams and Colonel Baker to United Industries' head office as soon as the admiral had explained to him the situation regarding the Alabama State.

United Industries' headquarters was a colossal complex that covered the majority of the island over which it sprawled. More akin to a city than a head office, the complex covered more than seventy-five per cent of the island's surface. After making the short trip down to the planet, the admiral's shuttle was directed to landing port beta, which was reserved solely for high-profile customers.

As soon as the pilot had cycled down the engines the port access hatch opened with a hiss of compressed air. As they stepped out of the shuttle, the admiral and his companions were forced to fight their way across the landing pad as stormy gusts threatened to blow them off their feet. Once they reached the terminal entrance a stony faced guard, rain running in sheets from his foul weather coat, ushered them inside. Having passed through a short featureless corridor the three naval officers entered the port's security office. After undergoing fingerprint and retinal scans, as well as blood screens, the admiral and his companions were issued with security passes and were escorted into the waiting room where they were met by a dour looking man in a dark grey suit.

'Admiral Pierce? Vice-admiral Adams? Colonel Baker?' he asked, without bothering to introduce himself.

'Correct,' the admiral replied.

'This way please; Doctor Milsen is expecting you.'

Without waiting for a reply he escorted them out of the waiting room, along several corridors and out into a large well light hall. Several dozen rails, inset into the floor, ran from a low platform that stretched across the length of the far wall into tunnel entrances cut into the other. The admiral's party were led two thirds of the way along the platform to where a small bullet-shaped vehicle stood waiting. Without saying a word their escort ushered them inside and took the controls.

'Please sit down,' he said. The three men complied, each settling into one of the forward-facing seats. With an acceleration that only the admiral seemed ready for, the small vehicle shot away from the platform and sped into the tunnel.

The journey lasted for about ten minutes, before they reached a small station with a long platform and a bank of a dozen lifts set into the far wall.

'Doctor Milsen is on floor one hundred and thirty-two.'

'Thank you,' the admiral replied before leading his companions out onto the platform. As they crossed the platform, making their way to the lift marked '100 – 150' the vehicle shot away from the platform, into the tunnel at its far end.

'Friendly chap,' Colonel Baker commented as they stepped into the lift.

'I doubt he was employed on account of his charming demeanour,' Vice-admiral Adams agreed.

'Floor one thirty-two,' the admiral said once the lift doors had closed and a blue panel had lit up on the wall. Like the shuttle from the landing port, the lift accelerated and decelerated sharply, taking only a few seconds to climb more than a hundred floors.

Floor one hundred and thirty-two was a world apart from the one they had just left. Richly furnished, spacious and comfortable, they were immediately greeted by a smiling receptionist.

'Good afternoon. Admiral Pierce, I presume?' she asked.

'That's right, Doctor Milsen should be expecting us.'

'He is indeed. His lift is along the corridor behind me,' she said, smiling.

'I can see why she was employed,' the colonel commented with a smile once they were safely out of earshot. The vice-admiral grinned. Admiral Pierce remained stony faced. 'That's what they'd have you believe, Grant, but I don't trust any of them.' The colonel was about to reply when the lift doors opened.

If the floor's foyer was richly furnished, the doctor's office was in a class of its own. Exquisitely reproduced classical wallpaper lined the walls whilst deep carpet covered the floor. Despite a haze of tobacco smoke, Doctor Milsen's office was an homage to Old Earth as it was in its glory days, now almost completely forgotten. The hum of the room's struggling air conditioner could barely be heard over the baroque music that was gently playing as the three men walked in.

'Ah, Admiral, Vice-admiral, Colonel, welcome.' Rising from a thick haze of cigarette smoke Doctor Milsen rose to greet them. Looking far older than his fifty-five years, the doctor was as lavishly dressed as his office was furnished. The finely patterned green frock coat he wore over his tailored suit lent him an air of aristocracy that suited him admirably. The only thing that detracted slightly from the look was the vents of his artificial lungs that protruded from his back. 'Please, Gentlemen, take a seat,' he said after shaking them each firmly by the hand.

As the three officers reclined in leather armchairs the doctor walked over to a cabinet and removed a decanter. 'Brandy?' he asked.

'Thank you, Doctor,' the admiral replied.

After pouring and serving the drinks the doctor sat himself down and lit another black cigarette. 'Now,' he began, taking a long drag, 'how may I be of service to my dear friends in the Federated States Navy?'

'Not to put too fine a point on it, we've lost one of our ships,' the admiral said.

'Destroyed?' the doctor asked as his lungs vented cigarette smoke into the room.

'Captured.'

'Go on.'

Over the course of the next half an hour the admiral explained the situation as it stood around New Jupiter and how they had come to lose the Alabama State. For his part, Doctor Milsen remained silent as the admiral talked and his companions expanded on this or that detail.

'So you doubt that you can re-take her in the same manner that she was taken in the first place? A fair assumption. Am I to understand that you are here to ask United Industries for help?'

'In a manner of speaking – yes,' the admiral admitted.

'Admiral, we are friends – you know this and I know this, but I'm afraid there isn't anything I can do. United Industries has a strict policy of neutrality – I'm sorry.'

'What if we could provide United Industries a service?' Colonel Baker asked.

'Colonel? I'm not sure I follow?' the doctor replied.

'Whenever we develop new naval assets we field-test them first, before commissioning them...' the doctor said nothing, but simply ground out his spent cigarette and pulled a fresh one from his coat pocket. 'Just suppose for a moment,' the colonel continued, taking a sip of brandy, 'that you had an asset in development that would benefit from a field-test. Don't you suppose that the Alabama State could provide you with an excellent opportunity?' The colonel met the doctor's gaze and held it until the other responded.

'You're proposing that United Industries *hire* the Alabama State for field tests – assuming we have any assets that require field-testing at the moment, that is?'

'Just so, Doctor. The fact that she's currently in Coalition hands is—'

'Unfortunate, Colonel; the ship is the property of the Federated American States and as such you have the right to hire her out to whomever you choose.'

'So the question is, Doctor, do you have any assets that you would like to field-test at the moment?' Vice-admiral Adams asked, looking over the rim of his brandy bowl.

'Do you know what, Gentlemen, I think we do.'

***

As the freighter Maria approached Port Vercuro a pair of naval tugs were dispatched to escort her to her assigned docking bay. The Maria was a huge slab-sided bulk carrier, the type that often transported water, processed ore, drive fuel and the like. On this occasion she was fully laden with process water bound for the electrolysis plant as well as a small quantity of machine parts.

'I'll never understand why the navy doesn't just buy its drive fuel like we do. Why do they insist on producing it themselves? I mean, they still buy in the mix gas for their atmosphere regulators,' Maria's helmsman asked no one in particular.

'You know how particular the navy is about the purity of the fuel they run their drives on,' the captain replied without taking his eyes off the view screen.

'Standard grade fuel has never has done us any harm, has it, Chief?' the helmsman replied.

'*Harrumph!* You've clearly never set foot in the engine room, Juan. We could do a lot worse than being a bit more selective about where we buy our fuel,' the chief engineer replied, grumbling.

'You know as well as I do, Thom', that we can't afford higher grade fuel. And besides, you've always been able to keep the old girl running!' the captain responded.

'We've just docked, Captain,' Juan reported.

'Very well, make ready to receive umbilicals and prepare the pumps. Oh, and tell Emilia that her hold crew can disembark once the machinery has been off-loaded and not a minute before – I know what they're like.'

'Aye, Sir.'

As the water was being pumped off the freighter the hold crew were busy unloading the machine parts, eager for as much shore leave as they could get.

'You've been quiet the whole trip, Gabriel, why don't you join us for a drink?' one of the hold crew asked another.

'Thanks, but I think I'll just grab a bite to eat and get some rest,' Gabriel replied. He was a young man who looked and acted every bit the void-virgin he was.

'Eager to get home, eh? The first trip out's the worst, trust me. It gets easier after that. Fair enough though, if that's how you feel. If you change your mind we'll be in the bar – don't worry there's only one us, civs are allowed in!'

'Thanks, I'll keep that in mind,' he replied before splitting off from the crowd of sailors heading for Port Vercuro's civilian bar. Once he was sure he was alone he slipped his I.D. pass into his pocket, darted down a side passage and headed back towards the warehouse where he had been unloading the Maria's consignment of machine parts.

'I'm sorry, but I think I left my pass on a loader,' he said as he approached the naval rating at the warehouse's entrance.

'How the hell'd you manage that, you idiot?'

'I'm sorry, it must have snagged on something – I'm pretty sure I know where it is.'

'Oh, all right, but be quick,' the rating replied as he keyed in the door's access code.

'Thanks – I won't be a second,' Gabriel replied as he slipped through the opening doors, the rating following close behind. After reaching the loader he had been operating he began to feign searching for his pass.

'Ah, here it is,' he said, withdrawing his hand from under the operator's seat.

'Wait, there's no pass in your—' Gabriel's strike was fast, but the neurotoxin was faster: the man was dead before he hit the floor.

'Hand? No, it was here in my pocket all along,' Gabriel said as he carefully removed the ring that concealed the micro-injector from his right hand. Taking a small penknife from the pocket of his coverall he made a small cut in the dead man's finger, massaged it and then reached down and licked up the blood that had welled up. A second or two after tasting the blood, Gabriel doubled over in pain and began shaking.

The transformation was shockingly rapid; first his hair changed and then his face – even the tone of his skin. By the time he stood up he was a perfect doppelgänger of the rating. Without hesitation he stripped the dead man, changed into his uniform and began searching the crates of machinery until he found one with a small mark carved into it – a mark that would be overlooked unless someone was actively looking for it. The crate itself was a standard pattern cargo container. After entering the correct code on the crate's lock, Gabriel, now Seaman Pablo Gomez, opened it and removed two cylinders marked 'Zystrom – pesticide'. After removing the cylinders he put his discarded coverall into the empty crate, followed by the body of the dead seaman. Having re-sealed the crate, he loaded the cylinders onto a small cargo truck and drove out of the warehouse.

No one paid any attention to a seaman transporting supplies across the port. No one questioned him as he made his way to the where the Alabama State, now the Almirante Pérez, was docked.

'You're late; she's about to put to space,' the rating at the airlock announced as he approached.

'I'm sorry – the civs took an age unloading, I got here as quickly as I could.'

'Damned civs – no sense of urgency – go on, but be quick about it.'

'Thanks,' he said as he boarded the battleship.

Once he was aboard he blended in with the rest of the ship's compliment as they made the vast vessel ready to put to space. Eventually he found his way to the ship's atmosphere regulation room. The room was empty and it was a simple enough procedure to replace two of the reserve oxygen cylinders with two cylinders he had brought over from the warehouse. All he could do now was wait, and so he blended in with the rest of the crew, never remaining in one place long enough to raise suspicion. On a ship the size of the Almirante Pérez finding a dark corner to hide away in was easy enough and so he didn't even need to bluff his way into a spare bunk.

Two weeks into the battleship's cruise Pablo retrieved a void suit from the ship's stores and made his way back to the atmosphere regulation room.

'Yes?' the corporal on duty asked as Pablo entered the room.

'Corporal, I'm here to—' Pablo was so fast that he had drawn his pistol and shot the corporal before he had fully turned from the control terminal. Working quickly Pablo locked the door and donned the void suit. Stepping over the dead corporal he cut power to the control terminal, triggering the reserve system to activate. Now he waited as the weaponised pesticide was pumped through the ship.

An hour later Pablo unlocked the door and stepped out into the corridor. A seaman lay a little way down the corridor looking for all the world like he was asleep. As he made his way to the bridge he passed other dead sailors, but paid them no more attention than he might an obstacle to be stepped over. Once he had reached the bridge he pushed the communications officer's corpse from his seat and sat down. Activating a secure channel he dispatched his report and waited for a reply. He did not have to wait long.

'Operative 16 respond.'

'Control, this is operative 16. Vessel secure. Awaiting instructions.'

'Operative 16, this is control. Mission complete. Await corvette U34.'

'Control, received and understood. Operative 16 over and out.' Other than restoring the ship's atmosphere regulator, there was little Pablo could do but wait for the United Industries vessel to arrive.

***

Several weeks later the Almirante Pérez docked at Archangel Spaceport and its United Industries skeleton crew disembarked. As a fresh F.A.S. crew was embarking, Admiral Pierce was in his office with Doctor Silvia Cranbrook who had come aboard the battleship from corvette U34 along with the skeleton crew.

An attractive woman in her mid-thirties, Doctor Cranbrook was the head of biomedical research at United Industries. 'Doctor Milsen was too busy to observe the results of the field-test first hand. I am here on his behalf,' she stated. Her dark grey suit and piercing eyes added to the palpable air of authority that she exuded, whilst her severe ponytail of strawberry-blonde hair accentuated it further.

'I'm pleased to meet you, Doctor,' the admiral began, offering his hand which she shook firmly. 'Doctor Milsen told me to expect you. You head the *project* that we have just field-tested, do you not?'

'I do, Admiral. I was able to review the results on my way up here. I am pleased to report that the field-test appears to have been a complete success.'

'Well considering that we got our ship back and your asset was undamaged, I'd say it was.'

'The return of the Alabama State was the ultimate objective, Admiral – we were also monitoring a number of other parameters during the test, the details of which are confidential; however, I feel confident we can progress with the next stage of development,' she replied, a hint of pride threatening to break through her measured, controlled countenance.

'When do you expect to put the asset on the market?'

'I'm not sure, Admiral, that's not my area – I have nothing to do with marketing.'

'Oh, well. I wish you every success with your work, Doctor.'

'And I thank you for the opportunity to conduct the test in such realistic circumstances.'

'Realistic circumstances? Thousands were killed – what a heartless bitch,' he thought. 'It wasn't our intention to lose the Alabama State in the first place, Doctor, but I'm pleased we could be of mutual assistance,' he replied as coolly as he could.

'I believe that will be all, Admiral,' she said as she turned to leave the admiral's office.

Once she had left, the admiral leaned back in his chair and let out a long breath. *'She's as cold and heartless as U.I. itself, still, I crossed the ice and didn't fall through, this time...*

Dr S. Fern

SEEDS OF TERROR

The survey vessel Forscher slipped silently through the void, its sensor array analysing the surrounding asteroid field. Huber Bergbau, the largest mining corporation in the European Union had sent Captain Dylan Edwards and his crew out to an unexplored region of The Field – the huge asteroid field some twenty light years from New Earth. It had been discovered by a United Industries exploration vessel shortly after New Earth had been colonised. Within a few years that monolithic corporation had dispatched a Quantum Tunneller to establish a stable wormhole between New Earth and the resource-rich region of the asteroid field.

The entire seven-man crew of the Forscher were asleep, except for Communications Officer Sofia Alesso who was on watch. The glow of the captain's console cast the delicate lines of her face in a haunting blue light.

'Rock... and void... and more damned rocks...' she thought to herself as she reached for her, now stale, coffee. The view of the star-field afforded by the glass bulb of the bridge was at once beautiful and hypnotising – in a word, peaceful. Closing her eyes, Sofia imagined she was back home in New Florence, enjoying her mother's famous carbonara.

Suddenly the impact alarm sounded, shattering the silence of the bridge. Sofia spilled the last of her coffee as the ship rocked violently to starboard. Stabbing the voice-activation button on one of the consoles she demanded a status report from the ship's computer.

'Outer hull breached, aft cargo hold,' the monotone voice replied.

'Integrity of inner hull, location aft cargo hold?' she asked, her mouth suddenly dry.

'No hull breach detected, location aft cargo hold.'

The young woman breathed a deep sigh of relief.

'Report,' the captain's voice came through the ship's communications system. He sounded groggy, only half awake.

'Captain, I'm reading a hull breach in the aft cargo hold but no de-pressurisation – the inner hull appears to be intact.'

'I'll be right there,' he replied before cutting the link.

Within minutes Captain Edwards was on the bridge wearing his void suit, his helmet locked securely to his thigh. The report of a hull breach had clearly shaken him. Sofia had served under the captain for several years and had come to learn that he had only one real fear; being voided.

'What's happened?' his voice was strained, edged with fear.

'Nothing critical, I don't think, Captain,' Sofia replied as she manipulated the external cameras, 'from what I can see we've been hit by a rogue asteroid. It appears to have punctured the outer hull but not the inner one. That's the only reason why the hull breach alarm would have sounded without the vacuum alarm also going off.'

Dylan visibly relaxed and slowly loosened the tight grip he had had on his helmet. 'Thank God. Okay, wake Liam, I want this repaired at once.'

Sofia raised Chief Engineer Wilson over the ship-wide communication's system.

'Yo, was'up?'

'Liam, are you high again?' Sofia asked.

'Well, no... I mean... just a little... Ah hell, Sofia, it's after hours... you know...'

'I know but we've got a hull breach in the aft cargo hold. I need you to go and check it out.' Sofia's tone betrayed her disapproval of the blind-eye her captain turned to Liam's cultivation and consumption of various psychotropic moulds.

'Babe, I can't breathe in the void, what do you want me to do?' the engineer asked, his voice sluggish.

'It looks like the outer hull's been breached but not the inner one – the vacuum alarm isn't sounding. I just need you to check that the inner hull is still sound before I send someone outside to remove whatever the hell it is that's impacted us.'

The communication's officer's tone sounded just a little strained as she attempted to relay the entire situation as succinctly as possible.

'Aah… safe as houses, Baby. I'll get right on it, no worries.'

Snorting in derision, she killed the link and turned to the captain.

'It's okay, Sofia, Liam's the best engineer I've ever sailed with; he may be high but you can trust him.'

'I'll be happier once I've got a definite report on the integrity of our inner hull, Sir,'

'Let's see the impact.'

'Here it is, it's… odd. It looks almost like it squashed or something as it hit the hull. It reminds me of…' Sofia's voice trailed off.

'Of what?'

'Oh, it's nothing, it's silly really. It's just that it reminds me of the buds that my mother used to pick in spring back on New Earth. Except that the petals weren't, well, you know, a space ship,' she replied, feeling more than a little foolish.

'You're right, that does sound silly,' the captain began.

'I know, I'm sorry—'

'But you're also not wrong. Wake Freya. I want her working on a way to remove that rock from our hull as soon as possible.'

'Sofia? Aah, Sofia?' Liam's voice, clearly unsettled, crackled across the communications link.

'Liam, go ahead. What can you see?' Sofia replied.

'Erm… well… you're not going to believe this but I'm fairly sure both hulls have been breached.'

'Make sense, Liam. You're in the aft cargo hold aren't you?'

'Yes, but—'

'So the inner hull can't have breached if you're in there, can it?'

'It can if you're seeing what I'm seeing. I'm going to seal the hold.'

'What? Liam, why?'

A long silence filled the bridge before the link crackled to life again, 'AAAGGHHHHHHHHHH!!!!!!!' and then silence.

'Liam! LIAM!' Sofia screamed into the microphone.

'Wake the rest of the crew! NOW!' Dylan ordered as she tried in vain to raise the chief engineer. 'And call up an internal view of the hold!' he snapped.

It didn't take long for the rest of the seven-strong crew to assemble. Sofia was trying to get a clear view inside of the aft cargo hold as Captain Edwards quickly filled the rest of the crew in on the situation as it currently stood.

'This is the best I can get,' Sophia was forced to admit after manipulating the image for some time. She called a live feed up onto one of the bridge's view screens. The entire screen was clouded out; evidently a duct had ruptured and had filled the hold with steam. For the briefest second Sofia was sure she saw movement in the steam-filled hold. No one else said anything so she kept quiet.

'It was nothing then, clearly. Besides, I've already embarrassed myself enough tonight… Mother's spring

bouquets! Honestly, get a grip, Sofia!' she thought. Although she didn't like to admit it, this whole situation was beginning to unsettle her.

'Right, Felix, you're with me – we're going to retrieve Liam from the aft hold. The rest of you, wait here.' The captain left the bridge along with his pilot.

A few minutes later the captain's voice came across the communications link. 'Liam's sealed the hold from the inside. We're going to need cutting gear to get in. We're heading to the maintenance bay to get the torches… and the heavy void suits, just in case,' the captain reported, stress again clear in his voice.

'Roger that, Captain,' Sofia replied.

Ten minutes passed in silence, and then they were plunged into pitch darkness. A second later the auxiliary battery kicked in to reveal a room full of worried faces.

'What happened?' the captain's voice burst onto the bridge via the communication's link.

'The ion drive shut down, Captain. Both the cooling and containment systems have failed.' Sofia's face was fixed on the captain's command console.

'Shit! Freya, what can you tell me about the rock that's stuck itself in us?'

'It looks like it's jammed fast,' she replied as she examined the external camera feeds, 'we're going to need to cut it loose. So long as the inner hull hasn't breached we should be able to burn it out and weld a patch over the hole. It won't be pretty but it will be enough to get us back home.'

'How long will the reserve power last?'

'About a week with standard usage,' Freya replied.

'Good, in that case I'm sending Felix back to you, he's the best void-walker on the ship. I want Felix and Sofia to go outside and cut that damned rock to bits, pull it from our side and patch us up. Freya, I want you to take the walkway over the holds to the engine room and fix the ion drive. Hannah and Victor, you're with me. Meet me in the maintenance bay, we're going to retrieve Liam.'

Sofia watched as the two geologists and the assistant engineer left the bridge. Suddenly she felt very alone.

'Sir, permission to set the communications system to Broad Report. I'd feel more comfortable if we were in constant contact with each other.'

The captain's reply was almost instantaneous. 'Yes of course. Do it at once.'

She quickly set the ship-wide communications system to Broad Report – the single channel setting that effectively connected every part of the ship. A single broadcast would now be relayed to every communications point, including the portable units attached to the crew's void suits. She had just finished when Felix entered the bridge.

'Ready?' he asked.

'Yes, I've just set the comms system to Broad Report,' she replied.

'Good idea. Now, shall we cut up a rock?' He asked, gesturing to the bridge door.

'Sure, after you,' she replied, '*Always so up-beat, sometimes that German drives me up the wall!*' she thought as they suited up before heading to the airlock.

'Captain, I've reached the engine room.' Freya's voice filled Sofia's helmet.

'Report, Freya. Can you see what's wrong?' the captain asked.

'Er, yes. But I don't know…' she began.

'We're on Broad Report, Freya, describe what you see,' Sofia said, trying to sound helpful. In all honesty though if she couldn't fix it, barring Liam, there wasn't a soul on the ship that would have much of a chance.

'Okay, Sofia. Well… the wall separating the engine room from the aft cargo hold has been breached in several places and there are these long, tentacle-like arms coming through. They almost look crystalline. They're clamped on to various engine systems, including the ion containment-field generator and the coolant system which explains why the drive shut itself down. There's coolant all over the floor. What are they, Captain? What are they?' Freya began to panic. 'If they're in *here* then... Have you got to Liam yet?'

'Freya, calm down. We haven't got to him yet, we're just about to start cutting through the hold door,' the captain tried to calm his engineer, though it was clear to Sofia that his nerves were beginning to fray too.

'Calm down? Captain these *things* have chewed right through a bulkhead, right through! They're *eating* the engine. THEY'RE *EATING THE DAMED ENGINE*! WHAT ARE THEY?!' Freya screamed. No one had an answer for her; no one dared to suggest the unthinkable. She began to cry. 'I'm scared, Captain; I don't know what to do.'

'Stay there, Freya, once we've cut through to Liam, we'll come and get you. Just... try to do what you can.' Dylan's tone was not at all confident.

'We've just got through to Liam,' the captain reported after a brief pause, clearly relieved. 'He's... Freya, get out of Engineering now! They're here in the aft hold, those things in the engine room; they're here too and they've got Liam.' The captain's relief turned to one of abject terror in the space of few seconds.

'Got him? What do you mean *got him*?' Freya sounded on the verge of hysteria.

'I mean *got him*. This stony tentacle... thing, it's eating him... whole. It's got a mouth like nothing I've seen before—' Freya's scream cut him off mid-sentence – an agonised scream.

'Freya!' Dylan shouted, 'Freya!'

Silence reigned in the engine room.

'Lamprey. It's a giant lamprey, or that's what it looks like,' Victor, the ship's assistant geologist, said, shock in his voice.

'Weapon's locker!' Hannah shouted, cutting across both of them.

Sofia was helpless, only able to listen as her captain and the geologists ran headlong through the ship towards the small weapon's locker behind the bridge. The more she looked at the huge rock that was jutting out of their hull the more the image of a flower came to mind. She could almost imagine the flattened sections of rock that were attached so firmly to the hull being the sepals of some kind of giant blossom. That idea was clearly ludicrous though, there were no petals or anything else vaguely reminiscent of a flower.

'*And besides, we're deep in the void for goodness' sake!*' She chided herself for loosing focus. 'Captain, this is Sofia, we have reached the asteroid and it looks... well, Sir, it looks more like it's clamped onto the hull than impacted it, Sir. I've never seen anything like it before. We're going to need some heavy cutting gear to remove it – whatever *it* is,' she reported.

'Received, Sofia. Get whatever you need, just get that thing off my ship. I don't care what it is, just get it off,' Dylan replied.

'Understood, Sir. We're returning to the ship.' She motioned for Felix to follow her. Together they slowly made their way back to the forward airlock. They were part way back when the staccato sounds of laser carbine fire came across the communication's system, filling Sofia's helmet.

'Captain?'

'Captain!' Sofia's call joined that of Felix's as they tried to raise their captain.

'We can't get to the aft cargo hold. They've reached the fore hold now... They're everywhere,' Hannah replied, panicked.

'Captain?' Sofia said, ignoring the shocked geologist.

'He's gone, Sofia. One of those lamprey-arms got him. He emptied an entire charge pack into it but...'

'Hannah, where are you?' Felix cut in.

'We're pinned at the far end of the fore hold, Felix. I don't think we can get out – they're everywhere,' Victor replied.

'You've got to try, Victor, both of you. If you can make it to the bridge we can vent both holds into space. We'd lose our ore samples and most of our supplies but we might be able to void it. There's no guarantee it will work though,'

'But it's worth a try?'

There was a long pause.

'Yes, it's worth a try,' Sofia said, supporting Felix's suggestion. 'Try to get to the bridge, we'll meet you there.'

'Okay, see you on the other side,' Victor replied.

The airlock re-pressurised with a hiss and Sofia led the way to the bridge.

'Victor, Hannah, we're back on board. What's the situation?' Sofia spoke into a wall-mounted communication's terminal.

Silence.

'Victor? Hannah?'

Silence.

'Felix, let's get to the bridge. Try and locate Victor and Hannah. I'll seal the cargo holds ready for voiding. I'll have to secure the engine room too,' she added as an afterthought.

As Sofia secured the ship's airtight doors ready for evacuation, Felix tried to locate the geologists.

'Crew scan complete,' the computer announced.

Felix hit the 'details' key on the touch screen.

'Communications officer, location, bridge. Pilot, location, bridge.'

'What about the others?' he asked himself. Beginning to panic he activated the computer's voice recognition system, 'Activate biometric locators.'

'Confirmed,' the computer replied.

'Locate Geologist King.'

'Chief Geologist Hannah King is not aboard the ship.'
'Locate Assistant Geologist Anderson.'
'Assistant Geologist Victor Anderson is not aboard the ship.'
'Shit!'
'Command not understood. Please re-phrase.'
Felix punched the deactivation button on the pad.
'Have you managed to find them?' Sofia asked as she crossed the bridge.
'No.'
'No?'
'They're gone. They're dead, Sofia,' the pilot replied, staring out into the vastness of the void.
'What do we do, Felix?' she asked, her voice little more than a whisper. The pilot turned to her, seeming to have recovered a little of his composure.
'We set the autopilot to detect the nearest ship, activate it, and seal every bulkhead on the ship – we should be safe here. The ship's reserve battery should have enough power if—' He was cut off mid-sentence as the bridge was plunged into darkness for a second time. This time the reserve battery had failed.
'What now?' Felix began.
'The life boat, it's our only chance; it's got its own power supply and life-support system.'
With a nod they cautiously left the bridge and began making their way towards the lifeboat. Suddenly the pitch-black corridor was filled with the tortured sound of metal tearing… or of it being torn.
'SOFIA! RUN!' Felix cried.
She did run, she left him for dead and she ran. She ran to the lifeboat, broke the emergency S.O.S. Panel and punched the large red button. She was about to switch the boat's system's to standby in order to conserve power when she remembered her *other* employer. Perhaps they would help. After all they had a vested interest in this survey mission too. Quickly she ordered the computer to copy the

contents of the Forscher's flight recorder. Once this was complete she sent it on an encrypted channel straight to her contact at United Industries. This done, she powered down all non-essential systems, removed a blanket from a locker and wrapped herself in it, praying that someone would find her before those *things* did.

***

'One life-sign, very weak, Captain.'

Captain Chandran of the Indian Navy frigate Ranjit nodded in response to the results of a ship-wide scan of the Forscher.

'The S.O.S. Beacon is still broadcasting?'

'Yes, Sir.'

'Very well. Bring us alongside. Have it brought into one of the holds and raise the nearest European ship. I'll not leave a vessel floating in the void for pirates to pick it clean like vultures.'

'Yes, Sir. Er, Sir?'

'Yes, Lieutenant, have you managed to raise the European Navy?'

'No, Sir. There's another ship just coming into range of our scanners. It's a big one.'

'Royal Indian Navy Vessel Ranjit, this is the United Industries bulk carrier U5475. You appear to be preparing to dock with the survey vessel Forscher.'

'Bulk Cruiser U5475, that is correct. We are responding to a distress call.'

'Negative, Ranjit, stand down. Survey vessel Forscher was leased by United Industries to Huber Bergbau and is therefore the property of United Industries. Please return to your original course.'

Captain Chandran looked across the bridge to another of his officers.

Dr S. Fern

'U5475 isn't a bulk carrier, Captain. I am reading energy spikes corresponding to multiple ion accelerator batteries and rail cannon silos.'

'Bulk carrier U5475, this is Captain Chandran of the R.I.N. Ranjit, we are standing down,' the captain replied before turning to address his bridge crew. 'The Forscher wasn't Indian and that was *not* a bulk carrier. Lieutenant Gutter, return us to our previous course.'

'Aye, Sir.'

***

Slowly and painfully Sofia re-gained consciousness. She found herself in an extensive medical bay.

'Ah, you're awake at last. You've been out for some time. How do you feel?' A short, slightly overweight doctor was leaning over her as she opened her eyes.

'Where am I?' she asked.

'You are on the Bulk Carrier U5475. We found your vessel drifting in The Field. It looks like you were hit by a rogue asteroid. Can you remember anything?'

Try as she might, she couldn't. She couldn't remember anything, not clearly; a few fragments of a nightmare but nothing more. She had always had an excellent memory and this troubled her.

'It's okay – it's a common side effect of severe oxygen deprivation,' the doctor began, noticing her look of consternation. 'When we found you you were almost dead. You had been drifting for a long time – you're lucky to be alive.'

The hiss of a door sliding open caught the doctor's attention. 'I have to go, but if you need anything, just ask one of the orderlies. You're fine now. Try to relax, it's all over.'

The doctor turned away from her to address whoever had just entered the medical bay. 'Ah, Doctor Cranbrook, I was told to expect you.' Sofia craned her neck, just able to make out a woman in her mid-30s who strode towards the doctor exuding an almost palpable air of authority. She had strawberry-blonde hair pulled back into a severe ponytail, and piercing eyes. She was at once intimidating and really rather attractive.

'What does she remember?'

'Nothing, nothing at all,' the doctor replied.

'You're sure?'

'Yes – her recall is effectively zero – vague recollections of a nightmare, but that's all.'

'Good. You will inform me the moment anything changes.'

'Of course.'

'That was not a request.'

'No, Doctor, I apologise.'

Dr Cranbrook turned from the doctor who had spoken to Sofia and approached a window. From her bed Sofia could only see the grey ceiling of what may have been a cargo hold.

'No one has been allowed near the Forscher?' Dr Cranbrook asked, addressing someone who was out of Sofia's line of sight.

'No, Ma'am—-'

'It's Doctor, not Ma'am. Good, see that it remains the case. No one is to enter the hold unless they're a member of my department,' she replied.

'Your department? Okay, sure. All this for an asteroid collision?' The unseen person tried his luck.

'Yes, my department – biomedical research. You're new at U.I., aren't you?'

'Yes M'... Doctor.'

'You're type don't last long – the human nose is short for a reason,' she snapped before turning and making for the exit. 'Asteroid impact? No; evidence of a terrible truth that must be concealed at all costs… we are not alone in the universe.' Sofia heard her mutter just as she left the medical bay.

Dr S. Fern

EXODUS

'And, so, it is on a note of optimism and hope that I formally close the fifth post-exodus global summit,' the conference convener said with a smile. The assembly hall in Brussels was packed with academics, leaders and countless other people who had been abandoned on Earth when United Industries lead the exodus to New Earth several decades previously. Each summit was a monumental undertaking to organise. Venues had to be prepared and secured, delegates had to be invited, have their identities verified and escorted across the globe, usually under heavy guard; Earth, or rather what was left of it, had become a savage, lawless planet in the wake of the departure of the world's governments. Nations had fractured with many degenerating into little more than perpetually warring tribal factions.

Despite this wholesale societal collapse there remained a small but significant remnant who held doggedly to the belief that a future was still possible for those who had been left behind. Often being forced to work in secret, they sought for ways to salvage what remained of the human race. At first it was hoped that further exodus vessels could be constructed to transport the rest of Earth's population through the wormhole that United Industries had bored, to New Earth. United Industries was the facilitator of the great exodus. Having worked itself into a position whereby it had a complete monopoly on off-world travel, the firm spent decades developing technologies that would permit mankind to leave its home-world for good. As the planet died mankind's many nations finally began to look to the future. By this time United Industries was in a position to offer a solution, to those who could afford it, and so alliances, coalitions and federations were formed. They turned to United Industries with blank cheques in their hands, begging the industrial superpower to save them, which it did.

It may have been possible to reach New Earth, the first couple of global summits eventually concluded, but it was agreed that they would not be welcome – history was replete with examples of racial prejudice and persecution. Another solution had to be sought. Many options were presented and discussed; biogenic regeneration, mass resettlement within the solar system, a second exodus to another New Earth and so on. It was eventually accepted that the Earth was dying and there was nothing that could be done to prevent it – the damage humanity had inflicted was too severe and too extensive.

The idea of city-ships was, at length, settled upon as the only plausible way forward. There was still sufficient expertise left on the planet to construct a fleet of colossal space ships, much larger than the huge exodus vessels that had facilitated the first migration to New Earth. These vessels would not seek to reach New Earth, nor even a similar planet, but would head out into deep space to begin a new chapter in mankind's history. The thrill of exploring the unknown, it was hoped, would break down the barriers of race, creed, religion and birth and draw people together with a common cause.

Initially, progress was painfully slow as a government had to be formed to head up the project and the factions that had taken control of the lunar settlement, and United Industries' gargantuan abandoned orbital shipyard, Olympus, had to be approached and talked round to joining. Eventually a government was formed, the lunar factions agreed to come together and construction finally began.

***

'Argh, Mate, that fuckin' 'urts!' The heavily tattooed man lying in the chair was grimacing and slick with sweat. He ran his free hand through his shock of ginger hair.

'You wanted the other arm pit done!' the tattooist replied.

'Yea, I know... how much longer though?'

'A couple of minutes – I'm almost done.'

A couple of minutes later the tattooist set his needle gun aside and gently rubbed some ointment over the fresh work. 'Alright, Henry, that's done. Have a look in the mirror,' he said as he began to dismantle and clean his equipment.

Henry stood up slowly and walked over to the mirror. 'Mate, that's wicked; I'm well 'appy with that,' he said, moving his arm around to see how the new piece looked from different angles.

'Yea, me too. It might need a touch-up though. Pop back when it's—'

'It'll be *fine,* Mate – it *won't* need touching up!'

'Captain, we've got to go,' a tall, stocky woman said as she entered the room. She then turned to the tattooist. 'Alright, Charles, how're you?'

'Phoebe, what's wrong? We're not due to depart for another day yet,' Henry asked as he gingerly put his T-shirt back on.

'They're locking the place down.'

'What, the port?' the tattooist, asked as he began to pack away his equipment into a sturdy metal toolbox.

'The whole lunar base – we're being kicked out – every ship registered out of Olympus. There's been an argument between the president and the prime minister apparently, but whatever the reason, security's moving through the port and evicting us; we've got to go – now.'

'Where's the Christina docked?' Henry asked.

'Bay 51, Mate,' Charles replied as he finished packing.

'Fucking hell, you'd better come with us – it'll take you an hour to get to her from here,' Phoebe said.

Charles grabbed his baseball cap from the corner of his bed, a suitcase from under it and followed Henry and Phoebe out of his bunk. 'Lucky I travel light, I suppose.'

The entire habitation wing was in chaos as the crews of a hundred different ships were herded to the docks by too few security guards.

'All this for a spat between a couple of suits?' Henry asked no one in particular.

'Those suits just so happen to be the president and his prime minister, Captain. You know as well as I do they've never got along,' she replied.

'Yea, they've been arguing ever since they formed the government. It's hardly surprising what with him being a hard-line Nomad and her being a die-hard Settler.'

'And the fact that she's a nutter,' Charles added.

'That too, but it was just an argument. Why—'

'It wasn't just an argument,' a short, wiry man interrupted as he shouldered his way through the crowd to their right.

'Allo, Ethan. What's that?' Charles asked, recognising his friend as he emerged from the crowd.

'I was saying it wasn't just another argument. Apparently President Jacobs finally brought Prime Minister Taylor to task over the Olympus audits. He wanted to know why the auditors had been refused access to various parts of the shipyard. One thing led to another and before long the whole chamber was back to arguing about whether we should head through the wormhole to New Earth, like the Settlers want or whether we should just pick a direction and go out and explore the galaxy, like the Nomads want.'

'They've been arguing about that for decades – what happened this time?' Phoebe asked.

'I'm getting there,' he replied. 'Anyway, the prime minister made the mistake of referring to Olympus as *her shipyard*, which pissed President Jacobs off no end.'

'Despite it being true,' Henry interrupted.

'It's true enough that she took it over after the exodus, once U.I. had abandoned it. But now, since the government's been running things, it's supposed to be answerable to *them*. Anyway, he called her a *bloody crook*, and she called him, and I quote, *a dickless faggot*, who was so afraid of confrontation that he'd rather wander the void for the rest of his life than take a chance at settling New Earth... at which point she drew a pistol and shot him.'

'Fuckin' 'ell!' Henry exclaimed.

'Quite. Anyway, Taylor said that she was taking a fleet to New Earth and whoever wanted to join her was welcome, so long as they could make themselves useful. Half the chamber followed her out of the chamber.'

'I guess that's it for the government then?' Phoebe asked.

'I'd say so; it looks like we're each going our separate ways. Your ship's registered at Olympus too, isn't is, Henry?' Ethan asked.

'Yes, Mate; why'd you think I'm heading to the docks rather than the bar?!'

'Fair point. We might want to pick up the pace a bit though – we don't—'

'Chill out, Mate; the security guards here are pussies. If they try anything I'll beat the shit out of them.'

'You, might, but I'm not really the—'

'It's okay, Baby, I'll look after you,' Phoebe said, putting a muscled arm round the smaller man's shoulders.

'Ha! You bet she will!' Charles laughed. Ethan blushed.

Eventually they reached bay 157 where Henry's ship, Void Dancer, was docked. Phoebe made her way down to the engine room to oversee the preparations for putting to space whilst the other three headed for the bridge.

'Contact the Christina and tell 'em we've got their assistant navigator and chief engineer on board; we'll send them over in a shuttle once were void-borne,' Henry ordered as soon as he stepped onto the bridge. 'How much fuel have we got, Izzy?'

'The pumps were shut off an hour ago, Captain; we're only at half capacity,' the engineer replied.

'Shit. Alright, once we've transferred Charles and Ethan head back to Olympus. We haven't got enough fuel to reach the Aussie' dock, load up, and make it back in one go. Bollocks! Fuckin' Nomads!' the captain cursed as Void Dancer slowly pulled away from the docking bay. At least once they got back to Olympus he would find out exactly what had happened and what the implications were.

***

Olympus Shipyard, as it was originally built by United Industries, was a colossal complex. The size of a small city, it was capable of berthing the entire fleet of exodus vessels built for the original migration to New Earth. As soon as Void Dancer arrived at Olympus they were hailed by the shipyard.

'They seem in a hurry,' Henry observed as the comm-link blinked on.

'Captain Henry Krämer of the freighter Void Dancer, this is Olympus Shipyard, please respond.'

'This is Henry – what's up, Olympus? You seem in a rush today,' the captain replied.

'Captain, you are to dock your vessel at bay three and proceed immediately to the C.E.O.'s office.'

'Alright, fair enough. Krämer out,' Henry replied before turning to his helmsman. 'I wonder what the old fella wants.'

'No idea, Cap, but we usually have to wait a sodding age to get a docking bay; I wonder where everyone is.'

'I guess I'll find out soon enough. I'm heading down to airlock two. Izzy, see that we're refuelled by the time I get back. I expect we'll be heading right back out, probably to the Aussie dock to pick the load we missed.'

'Righto, Cap.'

Henry was admitted to the C.E.O.'s office immediately upon his arrival.

'Captain Krämer, please come in. Take a seat,' the C.E.O., an ageing man with thinning hair, said as Henry entered the sparsely furnished office. Doing as he was bade, Henry sat down in one of the two metal chairs that faced the C.E.O.'s desk.

'If this is about me not picking up the Aussie' load there wasn't anything I could do – they wouldn't give us enough fuel – we wouldn't have made the return trip,' Henry protested, trying to pre-empt the dressing down he was sure was about to come his way.

'It's not about the ore shipment, Captain, I'm well aware of the situation you found yourself in on the moon. You've heard what's happened, I take it?'

'If you mean about the prime minister shooting the president, yea, I heard about that – that's what kicked off the trouble on the moon.'

'That's not what I mean, Captain. The incident in the governmental chambers was just a spark. The prime minister has taken back direct control of Olympus and is preparing to lead a fleet through the wormhole to New Earth.'

'It's finally happening then? Who's she taking with her?'

'Anyone who can make themselves useful. Everyone on Earth that's had a hand in supplying this shipyard is guaranteed a berth and she's taking on additional skilled labourers where she can.'

'What about everyone else? I thought the plan was to take *everyone* with us?'

'That was the Nomad's idea, not ours – let *them* take the waifs and strays.'

'To be fair—'

'To be fair, *nothing*, Captain. Do you want a couple of hundred extra mouths to feed on your ship? Do you want to have to carry that much dead-weight around with you wherever you go?'

'Well no, not really.'

'Answer me this, Captain, how did you come to command your own ship? Was the commission handed to you or did you have to earn it?'

'Well, I earned it.' In fact Henry had not earned it as such; he had won it one night in a game of poker. When the loser had confronted him about it the following morning Henry beat him so badly he spent the next six months in traction.

'Exactly, so how would you feel if we suddenly had a load of freeloaders coming up from Earth asking to be bunked and fed? Would you welcome them with open arms? Would you be happy to have your wages slashed in order to look after them?'

'Now that you put it like that, no – fuck 'em.'

'I couldn't have put it better myself, Captain, but I didn't call you here to bring you up to date on current affairs. You may have noticed that the docking bays are somewhat emptier than is usually the case.'

'Yea, we noticed that on our way in.'

'As soon as it was announced that the Settler-Nomad split was official I was given orders to protect our supply lines by any means necessary.

'I don't follow – what's that got to do with the empty bays?'

'Every vessel that arrives at Olympus is being armed – we need to be able to defend ourselves. I want you to bring your ship to hanger 132; there's a berth waiting for you there. I have arranged for quarters to be made available for yourself and your crew – I expect the work to take about a month.'

'A month? What kind of armament am I getting?'

'Here're the plans for Void Dancer. Take a look for yourself,' the old man said as he called up freighter's refit plans on the desk monitor.

Henry's eyes widened and his mouth dropped open. 'Fuckin' 'ell... I'm surprised it'll only take a month,' he gasped.

'All other work has been halted while the refits take place – even on the city-ships.'

'No wonder she didn't allow the auditors access to the entire shipyard. If they'd have found out she had so much weaponry stockpiled—'

'It would have been a disaster for us Settlers. Fortunately they didn't find out and once the city-ships are finished we can leave this godforsaken planet behind for good.'

'How long will it take to complete them?'

'Current projections are suggesting completion of all twelve vessels within the year, so long as supplies from Earth aren't interrupted.'

'You give me Void Dancer like it shows here,' Henry began, pointing at the displayed blueprint, 'and I *guarantee* those pansy-arsed Nomads don't interrupt a single supply run I make.'

'I'm glad to hear it, Captain. Oh, and one last thing before you go, I'll be assigning you additional crewmen to operate your weapons systems. I suggest you take the next month to integrate them with your current crew.'

'Not a problem.'

'Excellent. In that case, that will be all, Captain; enjoy your stay at Olympus.'

'I intend to – thanks.'

***

The Void Dancer's compliment of six officers and twenty-four crew were assigned quarters in one of the shipyard's self-contained habitation units. Before he let them officially disembark, Henry called the crew together in the ship's galley.

'Right, a couple of things. You've probably all heard by now that the split between the Settlers and the Nomads is official.'

'So we're going to New Earth then, Cap?' the ship's second mate, asked.

'Yea, Sylv, we're going to New Earth, but only once the city-ships have been completed.'

'And I guess the Nomads aren't just going to sit back and let us finish 'em?' Phoebe asked.

'Probably not, which is why they're upgrading the Void Dancer to make sure we can keep getting the supplies through to Olympus.'

'When you say *upgrade*, Captain, what exactly do you mean? Faster engines – something like that?' the ship's second engineer asked.

'Not quite, Jack; they're arming us.'

'You mean they're giving us guns?' one of the bridge hands asked.

'*Big* guns – trust me – I've seen the plans. We're also getting some new crew to operate them.'

'How long is this going to take?' another of the bridge hands asked.

'About a month, so we're all off duty until then. As soon as they assign our new crew I'll call you together to meet them. Right, that's it, you're all off duty except Fran. I need you to run the ship over to hanger 132 – that's where they'll be working on her.'

'No problem, Captain,' a middle-aged woman, with black hair streaked with silver, said.

It took about an hour to reach hanger 132 from bay 3. As they approached the hanger a pair of tugs were dispatched to guide them to their berth. The hanger was enormous; large enough to house a dozen large freighters like Void Dancer. Once the ship had successfully moored the captain signed her over to the team who were responsible for her refit and, along with Francesca, was escorted back to their habitation unit.

The habitation unit was more like a small town than anything else. There were shops, restaurants, bars – pretty much everything an off-duty space-farer could want. By the time Henry and Francesca arrived at their assigned berths there was no sign of the rest of Void Dancer's crew. Most of them would be found in the bar, Henry knew, except for his chief engineer: Phoebe would be searching for a bordello that catered to her tastes.

Around three weeks into their stay at Olympus Henry was awakened one morning by his door chime. He untangled himself from the woman who was still fast asleep in his bunk; the steward's assistant from the Spirit of Orion, he recalled with some difficulty as he shuffled towards the door. 'Who is it?' he asked via the intercom.

'Commander Rashid Hasanov, your new tactical officer, Captain. I am here with the Void Dancer's new tactical crew. We were told to report to your quarters.'

Just a minute,' Henry mumbled. He looked around the bunk for a moment before shuffling over to the bedside and retrieving a pair of underpants from the floor. He pulled them on and opened the door. Commander Hasanov was accompanied by four other men and three women.

'I'm sorry to have woken you, Captain, I had expected to find you…'

'Yea, no – it's okay. Give me half an hour and I'll meet you in Joe's,' Henry replied, rubbing the sleep from his eyes.

'Er, okay, we'll see you then,' the commander said as Henry shut the door on them and stumbled back to bed.

About forty-five minutes later Henry arrived at Joe's café. He kissed the woman he'd spent the night with, whose name he still couldn't recall, and walked over to where the dour commander and the others were waiting for him.

'So you're my new crew then?' he said as he waved a waitress over.

'That's right; I am commander Rashid Hasanov and these are my deck officers, Lieutenants Vega, Martin and Johnson,' the commander began, introducing two of the men and one of the women who were sat with them. 'This is chief engineer Arthur White and assistant engineers Camila Díaz and Claire Ivanov,' he concluded.

'I've already got engineers—'

'I doubt your—'

'Yea,' Henry interrupted the commander as the waitress arrived to take their order. 'I'll have Big Joe's full breakfast with extra black pudding, a mug of tea and toast as well as fried bread.' The waitress wrote down his order and turned to the others.

'We've already eaten, thank you,' the commander said, a note of distaste in his tone.

'Suit yourself,' he said as the waitress walked off. 'But, I tell you, this is the best place to come after a heavy night – hands down.'

'As I was saying, you'll need my engineers, Captain, because I doubt your current crew can maintain the new systems that are currently being fitted to your ship.'

'Fair point. I'd like you lot to meet the others before we leave Olympus. My crew are a family, Commander – fairly dysfunctional at times, to be honest, but a family nonetheless. It'll take you a bit of time, but so long as you're not a complete load of dickheads, I'm sure you'll fit in just fine.'

'That's a good idea, Captain. Where are your crew at the moment? Would it be possible to meet them this morning?' Arthur asked.

'They're probably nursing splitting hangovers, like me – we were out fairly late last night.'

'So it seems,' Lieutenant Johnson said as Henry accepted a plate of toast and a mug of tea from a waitress.

'I'll give you some advice, all of you,' Henry began between mouthfuls of hot buttered toast. 'You'll need to loosen the fuck up if you're going to fit in on Void Dancer. You all look like you're walking around with broom handles up your arses – chill out a bit.' The waitress returned with a large plate piled high with fried food. Henry tucked into the breakfast, much to the distaste of his new crew. 'How long until the work's finished?' he asked after a large swallow of tea.

'The work should be complete within the week – the hardware's all in place,' the commander answered.

'I think it'll be best to leave it until tomorrow before introducing you lot to the crew – they'll shoot me if I wake them any time soon! How about we go over to Void Dancer after I'm finished here and you show me the new systems?'

'That sounds like an excellent idea,' Arthur said. 'I'd like to spend some time getting acquainted with the systems while before we're void-borne.'

'It's certainly a good use of time considering the circumstances.' the commander replied as Henry shovelled an entire rasher of bacon in to his mouth. The commander and the rest of his crew waited in silence whilst Henry cleared his plate, mopped up the sauce and egg yolk with the last slice of toast and downed the last of the tea.

'Let's go, shall we?' he said as he grabbed a passing waitress and pressed what he owed into her hands.

***

'She's put on a bit of weight, hasn't she?' Henry remarked as the shuttle cleared the hanger doors and Void Dancer came in to view. The freighter's keel was significantly deeper than it had been. Her dorsal line had been raised so that only the command deck of her bridge protruded above it. 'I'm not being funny, but you *did* say she'd be getting guns…'

'Captain Krämer, your vessel is a freighter, not a warship; she's not supposed to be armed—' Commander Hasanov began.

'You are takin' the piss, right?'

'She isn't *supposed* to be armed, but she is – her weapons are concealed. Take a look here.' The commander gestured to the forward section of Void Dancer's newly deepened keel. 'You see that pair of hatches at the front of the new keel? They conceal a pair of rail cannons.'

'Oh yea; I s'pose they'll blend in with the rest of the hull once they've been painted...'

'That's the idea, Captain.'

'So what've you got hidden away along the dorsal line? I can see the new hull plating clear enough but I can't make out any hatches or anything.'

'That's because there aren't any, Captain. Six laser cannons in twin mounts have been installed; two forward of the bridge and one aft. False panels are concealing them from view at the moment.'

'That's something else, Mate – that's proper cunning!' The captain grinned as the shuttle docked with Void Dancer. He'd never owned more than a pistol before, and he'd had to 'lose' that after a particularly nasty bar brawl one night. Now however he found himself captain of an armed merchantman, and a heavily armed one at that.

Aboard it was a hive of activity. The engine room looked like a bomb had gone off in it, but Arthur assured him that the majority of the work had been completed – the power supplies to the weapons systems had already been installed. It was now simply a case of upgrading the reactor control systems to cope with the additional systems that they would have to manage.

'Just make sure you get all this cleared up before Phoebe sees it – she'll go ballistic otherwise,' Henry commented as they turned to leave. There wasn't much to see of the rail cannon emplacement – just four banks of huge capacitors and a pair of enormous auto-loaders.

'So all this is controlled from the bridge then?' Henry asked.

'That's right, Captain, both the rail cannons and the laser batteries are controlled from fire control, on the bridge,' Lieutenant Vega replied whilst the commander and his engineers talked with a couple of technicians.

'Everything alright?' Henry asked as they made their way to inspect the forward laser batteries.

'Yes, Captain, I was just checking on the progress of the work. It's just as Arthur was saying, the majority of the work has been done, there's just a few final bits and pieces to do before they take her out and put her through her paces on the test ranges.'

'I'd like my myself and my officers to be there for that.'

'That shouldn't be necessary, Captain; my officers and I will be operating the weapon systems, and my engineers will be responsible for their maintenance.'

'Yea, but *I'm* the captain and *I'm* in charge, and when I'm not on duty my bridge officers are, okay? And besides, Phoebe and Jack are in charge of the engine room, so they'll need to be there too.'

'Fair enough, Captain, I'll let you know when the void trials are due.'

'Thank you,' he replied, not a little sarcastically. 'So this is one of the forward laser turrets?' The turret itself was large but inside it was claustrophobic; the lasers themselves were huge and their power supplies no less so. 'What're those for?' Henry asked, pointing at a pair of small fold-away seats which were mounted one to the right hand side of each laser.

'They're for sitting on,' Claire replied.

'Don't get fuckin' cocky with me, Girl; I know they're for sitting on. I was asking why there'd be seats when it's all meant to be run automatically from the bridge.' Claire met his gaze and returned it, the tension in the room mounted rapidly.

'They're in case the battery needs to be fired manually,' Arthur replied quickly, trying to defuse the situation.

'*Thank you*, that's all I wanted to know.'

'They're just there as a precaution; the fire control network is well shielded,' Camila put in.

'I hope so; fuck sitting in that little box in the middle of a shoot out…' Henry muttered as they made their way to the bridge.

The bridge's command deck had been extended and now ran the entire depth of the bridge. Behind the captain's chair a large workstation had been installed that was entirely circular barring a 20° sector through which the operator entered.

'You've got more monitors than me!' Henry laughed, gesturing to the bank of monitors that had been installed on the bridge's rear wall.

'Whoever's on duty needs to be able monitor every weapons system as well as have access to appropriate tactical plots,' Lieutenant Martin replied.

'Is there a manual or something I could look at?' Henry asked.

'Why would you want one, Captain? I assure you, we are *all* of the highest calibre – we wouldn't have been assigned to you if we weren't,' Commander Hasanov replied.

'*Yea, like the C.E.O.'s going to assign the* best of the best *to a freighter crew. And besides, I don't trust you lot yet.*' he thought, before replying, 'I like to know my ship, Commander; what she's capable of and what she's not – I'm not trying to do your job for you.'

'I'll see that you have a copy of the new systems' specifications by the end of the day.'

'Thanks.'

'*And* I'll *see that Phoebe gets a copy too.*' The journey back to the habitation unit was undertaken in silence. None of the captain's new crew made any attempt to make conversation – they were die-hard navy wannabes, like so many that worked full time at Olympus, and he was just a freighter captain.

Once Henry had made arrangements for his new crew to meet the rest of Void Dancer's compliment at Little Linda's Bar the following evening he made his way to his quarters. He desperately needed a shower, some painkillers, and then to go to bed – the last few hours had brought his hangover back with a vengeance.

***

Commander Hasanov was as good as his word. The following afternoon Henry received a copy of the new systems' specifications. After obtaining what passed for chicken and chips from the food dispenser at the end of the corridor, he retrieved his last bottle of genuine Earth-produced tomato sauce from his locker and settled down to begin reading. The manuals were dry reading but he forced himself to read everything, except the technical parts that were beyond him. He was just putting the last manual down – U.I. Mk2B Fire Control System – and letting his heavy eyelids close when his door chime jerked him fully awake. Putting the volume to one side he stood up, crossed the room and opened the door.

'You ready, Cap?' Phoebe asked. The chief engineer was dressed in a brightly coloured, geometrically pattered mini dress and bright red deck boots.

'What? Oh, we're meeting the new lot at Linda's later on. What time is it?'

'Half five, yard time.'

'Really?'

'Yea. What've you been up to all day?'

'Reading through spec manuals for the ship's new systems.'

'Sounds like fun. Come on or we'll be late.'

'Just a minute.' Henry retrieved the manuals from his quarters before joining Phoebe in the corridor. 'I want you to read these as well.'

'Now?'

'No, not now – before we take her out onto the test ranges.'

'When's that likely to be?'

'A couple of days' time probably.'

'Okay, no problem. Just a mo – I'll drop these off in my quarters.' Phoebe took the manuals from Henry, turned, and stomped off down a side corridor. Henry heard the thud of her deck boots when she returned before he saw her.

'There's no need to run, mate; it's not as if we've got a table booked or anything.'

'I know, but I fancy a beer, and besides I'm looking forward to meeting our new crew.'

'You *need* a beer? We were out two nights ago, and from what I remember you were fairly tanked *before* you went in search of company.'

'Yea, but now it's *tonight* – a whole different night!'

'Just remember, were mainly going out to get to know the new crew – not for you to get trashed and laid!'

'What are you saying?!'

'Just that I know what you're like when you've had a few – you disappeared quite early the other night as I recall!'

'About eleven I think. How was the rest of the night?'

'I barely remember. You?'

'Good, thanks. There's a couple of new faces in Cassiopeia's.'

'Any you liked the look of?'

'A couple; a guy called Leo and a girl called Paige.'

'A couple? You'll have spent everything you've earned before we're back in the void.'

'Not really. I fixed their air conditioner; I booked Leo and they threw in Paige as payment.'

'You really are a whore sometimes!'
'*I'm* the one that's paying...'
'For *two* in one night!'
'At the *same* time...'
'I don't know why I'm surprised anymore!'

Little Linda's Bar was already beginning to fill up. As they approached Phoebe strode off and shouldered her way through the growing crowd to the bar.

'Captain!' Commander Hasanov was standing at a table at the far end of Little Linda's. By the look of it a number of his crew had already arrived. Henry left Phoebe at the bar and went over to join them.

'How did you manage to get served so quickly?' the commander asked when Phoebe arrived a few minutes later with her and the captain's drink.

'Do you really need to ask that question, Commander?' Francesca, Henry's first mate, asked.

Rashid Eyed Phoebe up and down. 'I see your point, Francesca.'

'You want to be careful, Commander, you cross Phoebs and she'll rip your cock off!' Jack laughed.

'Screw you, Jack! He's just jealous, Commander, because I'm above him.'

'I wouldn't mind that at all!' the young second engineer replied.

'You'd get broken, Darling!' Phoebe replied with a wicked grin.

'Commander Hasanov,' Henry interrupted. 'May I introduce my chief engineer, Phoebe. Phoebe, Commander Rashid Hasanov, Lieutenants Vega, Martin and Johnson and engineers Arthur White, Camila Díaz and Claire Ivanov.'

'Welcome to the Void Dancer.'
'Who's missing?' Henry asked.
'A couple of the engine room guys and a few others,' Sylvia replied after looking over the long table for a moment or two.

'Josh's in minor injuries getting signed off – he'll be here later on,' Francesca added.

'What's wrong with your third mate, Captain?' Rashid asked.

'Oh, he had an accident a couple of nights ago,' Henry replied.

'Yea, jousting!' Samuel, the ship's chief cook, added.

'Jousting?' Claire asked, incredulous.

'We'd had a few meltdowns—'

'Meltdowns?' Arthur asked.

'One of Linda's cocktails – lethal! Anyway, we'd had a few of them and Ali suggested jousting – go on, Ali – it's your story!'

Ali, the ship's junior engineer continued the tale. 'I'd seen these two small cargo loaders earlier in the day. They'd been parked at the end of a corridor a little way from here. Anyway, as Sam' said, we'd just had another round of meltdowns and I had this idea that we could liberate a couple of brooms and a couple of container lids and joust along the corridor.' Claire's mouth dropped open. 'It was a great idea, and Josh was up for it so off we went! Josh was two points up when…' Ali broke down laughing.

'When his broom came off Ali's shield, caught in the loader's cab frame and he veered off right into a support stanchion!' Samuel finished Ali's story.

'So what did you do?' Arthur asked.

'We pulled him from the wreck, ran like hell and dumped him at the corner of Linda's – made it look like he'd taken a fall or something!' Henry replied.

'Are you aware—' Claire began.

'So?' Phoebe interrupted. 'We're not yard crew; the same rules don't apply to us – or to you now!' Claire's response was drowned out as the whole table raised their drinks and shouted 'VOID DANCER!'

'Josh!' One of the bridge hands shouted a couple of seconds later.

'I guess I owe a round!' an old man with long thinning grey hair said as he set a large tray of drinks on the table. The cheer that went up as the Void Dancer's third mate passed round shots of a clear spirit was deafening. It was when they all toasted Josh together that Henry was confident that the new additions to his crew would fit in well with the rest. The rest of the night was an alcohol-fuelled haze. No one could recall at what point Phoebe and Claire disappeared, let along how any of them managed to get back to their respective quarters.

***

Henry was gingerly beginning his breakfast at Joe's when Phoebe and Claire arrived, looking equally fragile. Claire was wearing the same dress she'd been wearing last night.
'Good morning, you too,' Henry managed a weak smile.
'Morning, Cap,' Phoebe replied.
'Morning, Captain,' Claire croaked.
'How d'you feel?'
'Not good,' Claire replied as she slowly sat down.
'Put it this way, you look like I feel, Cap,' Phoebe answered.
'That bad, eh?'
'Yea.'
'Have you seen anyone else yet?' Claire asked as she waved over a waitress.
'Only Josh – that man's a machine – he's been and gone already. I don't know how he does it.'
'Years of practice.'
'Yea, but to be fair, Phoebs, he should be dead by now!'
Claire began to laugh but grimaced as pain shot through her head. Phoebe gave her a pained look and took the engineer's hand in hers. 'You'll be alright once you've had something to eat and the painkillers kick in.' She turned as the waitress approached. 'Two coffees, toast and two plates of egg and bacon, please.'

Lieutenant Vega arrived whilst the women were waiting to be served. 'The commander not here?' he asked as he slowly sat down.

'I don't think we'll be seeing him today,' Henry began with a mouthful of hash brown. 'By the time you lot left he'd finished the bar's bottle of starblood and was singing along to some right old shit – I can't remember what it was.

'Yea, I remember earlier in the night Francesca warned me not to touch that stuff. How did she describe it? Like a cross between medicinal alcohol and dragon fire, that's it,' the lieutenant said as he joined the other three at the table.

'She's right n'all – that stuff'll fuck you right up – trust me,' Henry replied between swigs of tea.

'You had some then?'

'One or two. That was enough though – I've learnt my lesson,' he replied as a waitress took the lieutenant's order.

'Bollocks, Cap – you'll do the same thing next time and you know it,' Phoebe said between mouthfuls of egg.

'Yea, I know – especially if Rashid has anything to do with it…'

Over the next half an hour a few more of Void Dancer's crew arrived. The rest remained in their quarters and weren't seen for the rest of the day. Henry had set out to introduce the new recruits to the rest of the freighter's crew. As far as he could tell he had succeeded in spectacular fashion.

***

Void Dancer pulled slowly away from docking bay three. The session on the test ranges had been successful and she was one of the first armed freighters to ply the shipping lanes between Earth and Olympus. There had been reports of blockades around all of Olympus' major suppliers' orbital docks. Henry had vowed to his crew that this run would be no different – they wouldn't be turned back by a few Nomad vessels blocking the approach lanes.

Beyond Earth: New Earth

The journey to Earth was uneventful and the crew were happy to get back into the routine of life aboard ship. It was always a welcome release to blow off some steam dockside but they were most comfortable aboard ship where their own rules applied and they didn't feel constrained by dockside rules, regulations and conventionality.

'Captain, you asked to be informed when we were approaching the Aussie' dock.' The intercom broke the silence in Henry's cabin. 'Captain?'

'Yea, okay – thanks – I'll be right up,' Henry replied, still only half awake. Crawling out of bed he crossed his cabin without bothering to turn on the light, the emergency light's dull green glow providing enough illumination to see by. He was about to step out into the corridor when he realised that he was naked except for a pair of threadbare underpants. Leaving the door to the corridor ajar he returned to his cabin's gloom and slipped into an old dressing gown and an equally old pair of slippers.

Henry stopped at the galley on his way to the bridge to pour himself a mug of the thick, black, heavily caffeinated drink that passed for coffee on the ship. Having filled a mug he lifted the lid of the urn and grunted. Setting the lid aside he retrieved a jar of dark brown powder, dumped several mugfuls into the urn, topped it up with water and replaced the lid. He arrived on the bridge several minutes later. Sylvia was on duty and she turned and smiled as he approached, her pink spiked hair almost as painfully bright as the glow from the console screens.

'Morning, Cap. It looks like we've got a blockade ahead,' she replied.

'Really? Let's have a look then,' he replied as he slumped down into the captain's chair.

'Here,' she replied as she called up a view on the bridge monitor whilst simultaneously pulling a strip of dried meat from one of the many pockets in her thermally-lined coverall.

'How can you eat that shit?'

'This? It's nice – want a piece?'

'No thanks – you've got no idea what it was before it became something that looks like it was scraped it off the galley floor!'

'So? It's tasty!' she replied, pushing another strip of cured meat into her mouth.

'Just keep it away from me and tell me what's in our way.'

'It looks like a line of bulk carriers. They've positioned themselves so that they're blocking the approach lane to the dock. If we try to go around them we risk colliding with the dock or entering the Earth-dock transit lanes, which I don't recommend.'

'Raise that carrier there.'

'Which one?'

'That one right in front of us – the big, fat, ugly one.'

'Righto, Cap – attempting to open a channel with the *big, fat, ugly one!*'

'This is Capitan O'Shea of the Emma Hall to the captain of the approaching freighter. I cannot permit you access to this dock, Captain. Please turn your ship around and leave.' The Emma Hall's Captain's voice was clear, crisp and entirely devoid of emotion.

'Captain O'Shea, This is Captain Krämer of the freighter Void Dancer. I need to get to the dock – I've got cargo to load, so I'd appreciate it if you'd just let me get on with my job,' Henry replied in calm tones.

'Captain Krämer, I'm afraid I can't do that – as you're well aware. Turn your ship around and leave, Captain.'

'Now just a minute; I've asked you nicely, but now I'm telling you – get out of my way.'

'Captain, I've made my position cle—'

'Just get out of the *fuckin'* way before I come over there and punch your *fuckin'* lights out, Mate.' Henry took a large swig of coffee and cut the comm-link.

'Captain, three other freighters from Olympus have just arrived astern of us,' Sylvia said in a low voice.

'Tell them to follow us in,' Henry replied just as the comm-link came alive again with Captain O'Shea's, now rather agitated voice.

'Captain Krämer, if you try to dock with us I will have you and your entire crew arrested. Do I make myself clear?'

'Clear as *fuckin'* crystal, Mate.' Henry cut the link with the Emma Hall, got up from his chair and walked round to the tactical station where Lieutenant Johnson was on duty. She swivelled in her chair as he approached.

'Abi', what'd you fancy?' he asked with a grin.

'Captain, I'm, er, not sure what you mean,' she replied, blushing.

'I'm sorry, I'm just messing around! We're going to punch through the blockade and I thought you'd like to choose how we do it.'

'Oh! Right! Ha!' she tried to hide her embarrassment behind several locks of her long auburn hair. 'It should really be your call, Captain.'

'I know, but I don't hit women.' The lieutenant's confusion was written across her face.

'The vessel that's blocking our approach to the dock's the Emma Hall,' Sylvia explained.

'Oh, right – you've got quite a sense of humour, Captain!'

'See, Sylvia, I'm a funny guy – even when I've only had three hours sleep!' Henry laughed.

'Yea, Right, Cap.'

'So, come on then, Abi', what's it gonna' be?'

'Well, Captain, seeing as we're approaching head on, I'd suggest using the rail cannons – we won't be in a position for a broadside with the lasers.'

In that case, Lieutenant, prepare the rail cannons; we're about to run a blockade.' Henry replied before returning to the captain's chair. 'Sylvia, ahead one quarter, and get me Captain O'Shea again.'

A few seconds later Captain O'Shea's voice filled the bridge. 'Captain Krämer, you can't hope to run this blockade successfully, trust me. Turn your ship around and go home.'

'Captain O'shea, I'm giving you one last chance to move your ship; I'm not in the mood to piss about.'

'Captain, surely you must see that you can't possibility—' Henry cut the comm-link again.

'Twat. Abi, shoot the bastard.'

'Aye, aye, Captain,' the young woman replied with not a little relish. There was a slight delay before the bow of the Emma Hall crumpled and then exploded. The flames were quickly extinguished as the bulk carrier voided its atmosphere to space.

'Sylv, take us through, all ahead full.' Henry drained his mug and put it down on the arm of his chair with a grin. It had been a long time since he'd killed someone, but it all came flooding back as he watched the Emma Hall drift out of formation, crippled. The thrill of it all, the rush, the intoxicating feeling of adrenalin flooding his system – he felt it all and found that it smothered any niggling guilt that he might have been feeling about sending an entire ship's compliment to their graves. '*I could get used to this…*'

Dock control were surprised, to say the least, when they saw Void Dancer and the other three freighters break through the Nomad blockade.

'It's good to see you, Void Dancer; it's been a bit quiet here lately,' the dock's loading master said over the comm-link. Evidently he chose not to comment on the manner in which the freighters had broken through.

'It's good to be here. We were due a month back, before the trouble started, but couldn't make it. Have you still got our cargo?' Henry asked, hoping it wouldn't cost him a small fortune in storage fees.

'We've still got it, Void Dancer, and before you ask, we're waiving the storage fees this time.' Henry breathed a sign of relief. 'Dock at berth six.'

The three vessels following Void Dancer were berthed in rapid succession and began filling their holds with all manner of supplies for Olympus. Void Dancer was loaded with finished components: mostly air-conditioning units, life-support modules and ion conduits. Once the cargo had been loaded Henry departed as soon as he was able to; not only was this a highly profitable cargo, but he was anxious to reach Olympus ahead of the other freighters and get his pick of the next run.

'Josh, what's the state of the blockade?' Henry asked as they were pulling away from the dock.'

'The Emma Hall's drifting. There's another ship moving to take her position though, Captain,' the old man replied.

'Right, punch it – get us through before they get there.'

'Can't we just do what we did before, Captain?' Lieutenant Vega asked from tactical.

'We could, Adolfo, but then we'd leave a great big hole for the others to slip through, and then if we're delayed, they might get back first and leave us with the shit runs – the ones that don't pay.'

'I see – that makes sense. I'll ready the lasers in case we need them.'

'Alright, but don't drop the panels – keep 'em hidden – we might not need 'em.'

'Aye, Captain.'

Josh accelerated Void Dancer to full speed and raced for the closing gap in the blockade. As the point they were heading for came into focus on the main view screen, it slowly became clear that they weren't going to make it through. The other ship, an old bulk carrier, had almost reached the Emma Hall's original position.

'Captain, shall I ready the weapons? We—'

'I can make it,' Josh interrupted. With his face glued to the main view screen, he called up a plethora of course projections, technical data and engine readouts with his left hand whilst his right searched the command console for the ashtray.

'Are you sure, Mate? That gap's getting a *bit* small for my liking,' Henry said, slightly nervous.

'Trust me, Cap,' the third mate replied, finally locating the ashtray and recovering his roll-up. As he pulled a lighter from the breast pocket of his tatty checked shirt and re-lit his cigarette, he put Void Dancer into a slight roll.

'You do realise we're still heading right for that ship?' The tension in Henry's voice had increased several notches.

'I see her, Cap – ugly bitch, ain't she?'

'Never mind what she *looks* like!'

As distance closed to several hundred kilometres Josh kept Void Dancer pointed directly at the other ship. Henry gripped the arms of his chair tightly, his knuckles white.

'Even if we miss the one we're heading for, you do realise there's another ship right above her, don't you?' Adolfo said.

Josh didn't reply, he just kept his face glued to the main view screen and dropped ash over the console. Void Dancer swept past the old carrier at 90°, starboard to starboard. They had almost passed the other vessel when Josh hammered the command console, rapidly inputting a number of commands. A second later the ship's thrusters fired and put her into a violent yaw, rolling her starboard side over the top of the other vessel. He cleared the vessel above by no more than a few kilometres.

The bridge crew breathed a collective sigh of relief as they passed into open space, except for Josh who just leaned back and rolled another cigarette.

'I need a drink, anyone else?' Lieutenant Vega and the three bridge hands all accepted the captain's offer. 'I'm not even going to bother asking you, Mate,' Henry added as he left the bridge. Josh grinned, his cigarette sticking to his lower lip.

Henry returned a few minutes later with six beers and passed them around. One of the bridge hands plotted a course back to Olympus, activated the autopilot and then joined the rest of the bridge crew as they celebrated.

Void Dancer was within two days' journey of Olympus when a corvette with strange markings pulled in front of her, forcing her to a halt. Henry was down in the engine room chatting with Camila.

'What is it, Fran?' he asked, speaking into a wall-mounted comm panel. 'Why've we stopped?'

'Another ship, Cap, a patrol ship with government markings, its forced us to a halt. They say we're charged with piracy and are here to arrest us and impound the ship.'

'What? Just a minute.' He turned to Camila, shrugged his shoulders and said, 'I've got no idea,' before turning and leaving the engine room. The face on the main view screen was that of a smart-looking middle-aged man in a light blue and white uniform.

'Captain, this is Commander John Hughes of the Government Defence Fleet. He'd like to talk to you,' Francesca said in her calmest voice as Henry entered the bridge.

'Who? What?'

'I am Commander John Hughes of the Government Defence Fleet and I am here to place you under arrest,' the commander began as Henry sat down.

'Sorry, Mate, but what the hell is the Government Defence Fleet?'

'It was formed in response to Prime Minister Taylor's treachery. The president may be crippled, but what he stands for is not – the great exodus will go ahead as he envisioned, and there's nothing that the ex-prime minister can do about it.'

'So Taylor wants to settle rather than wander the void – what's that got to do with us?'

'You are Captain Krämer and this is the Void Dancer, is it not?'

'Yea, so.'

'You are registered as operating from Olympus Shipyard, and are therefore supporting the traitors. That in itself is grounds for me to impound your ship, but you are also charged with piracy. Captain—'

'Traitors, that's a bit rich isn't it? Some of us don't much fancy the idea of wandering the void until we die of old age. How's that treason? And where'd you get piracy from?' Henry laughed.

'The Olympus Shipyard is where Taylor is building her fleet. You are registered there and are therefore guilty by association. If of course you wish to—'

'Bullshit, Mate, that's—'

'You are also charged with piracy, Captain,' Commander Hughes raised his voice and spoke over the captain. 'You are charged with destroying the government-registered carrier Emma Hall, though I can't see how, and seizing supplies bound for the lunar shipyards. I will accept your surrender, Captain; you will be given a fair trial. I am a reasonable man.'

Henry sat in silence for a moment or two, unable to form a coherent response. 'That's... that's bullshit,' he finally managed.

'No, Captain, it's the law.'

'Well it's not *my* law, Mate, so I suggest you piss off.'

'I'm not going anywhere, Captain, not until I have placed you and your crew under arrest.'

'Then we've got a bit of a problem, Mate.'

'No, Captain, *you've* got a problem. I'm faster than you, and more manoeuvrable. I've got a full platoon of armed enforcers on board, and I'll board you if I have to.'

'Well that settles it then, doesn't it?'

'I'm glad to see that you too are a reasonable man, Captain. Please prepare to—'

Henry cut the link. '*Reasonable man*? Francesca, if I ever start becoming *reasonable*, shoot me. In the meantime, who's at tactical?'

'Me, Captain,' Rashid replied.
'Shoot him, Rashid.'
'Aye, Captain.'

As the patrol vessel swung around and prepared to dock with Void Dancer's starboard docking ring, the panels concealing the freighter's laser batteries slid away. The three turrets swung round and raked the smaller vessel with high energy volleys from stem to stern. Fires flared up before guttering and dying as the ship's atmosphere bled into space until she was nothing more than a drifting hulk, devoid of power and life.

'Get us moving again, Fran', I don't want to be overtaken.'

'Righto, Cap.'

***

Just over forty hours later Void Dancer docked at Olympus Shipyard and unloaded her cargo. Henry left the unloading to his first mate and headed straight for the loading master's office to collect his next assignment.

The loading master was a portly man of middle years whose comb-over did little to hide his receding hairline. 'I should have known you'd be the first through a blockade, Krämer,' he said as Henry entered his office.

'How'd you hear about that? We've only just docked.'

'Everyone's heard about it; the government's furious. It was bad enough when the prime minister seized control of Olympus and announced that we were going through the wormhole regardless of any Nomad ideas to the contrary, but now with you attacking one of their ships... They've ordered your arrest, did you know that?'

'Yea, they sent a patrol ship out to bring me in.'

'How did you convince them not to?'

Henry raised his eyebrows. 'Do you really need to ask?'

'Oh, no. You didn't, did you?' The loading master's jaw dropped open.

'Let's just say there's one patrol ship that won't be bothering anyone again. Now, what've you got for me?'

'Oh, this is bad, Henry, this is very bad—'

'Taylor armed us for a reason – to keep the supplies coming in. What did you expect was going to happen?'

'I know, I know. I can see all this getting very out of hand very quickly, that's all. You'd better not go back to the Aussie' dock any time soon,' he said as he scanned through a number of lists on his console screen. 'Here, there's a shipment of process water that's due for collection.'

'*Process water*? Come on, Mate, that's a shit job. You must have something else.'

'A *shit job*, meaning it doesn't pay as well as your last one? No, it doesn't, but it'll keep you out of the major shipping lanes, and hopefully, trouble. From what I hear construction's almost complete.'

'How do you know?'

'I see everything that comes into the 'yard. There are a *lot* of deliveries of process water scheduled. That can only mean one thing.'

'They're getting ready to fuel-up.'

'Exactly. I'd say we'll be leaving in, oh, say, a couple of weeks.'

'I hope you're right.' Henry picked up the job details and returned to Void Dancer, eager to be void-borne again as soon as possible.

The loading master was right – Taylor's fleet began to put to space two weeks later. As it formed up, the shipyard began to empty as everyone and everything was transferred to the colossal city-ships and smaller auxiliary vessels. It took around another month for all those on Earth that had managed to secure themselves passage to leave the planet. During this time Void Dancer, like a number other freighters and cargo vessels, became a ferry as it transported hundreds of thousands to the waiting fleet. The Nomads didn't interfere, deciding that it would be easier to simply let those who wanted to, leave. Once the Settler fleet had departed, work on the Nomad city-ships could begin again – they could even recommission Olympus if they needed to.

Eventually the enormous settler fleet was ready to leave Earth for good. It was with very few regrets that Henry and his crew turned Void Dancer away from Earth for the last time and moved into position behind the city-ship Dublin as it prepared to enter the wormhole.

***

In the main control room of Liberty One – the large United Industries space station that had once been New Earth's outer-most moon – an alarm began sounding.

'What is it, Peterson?' a dour man with a long, thin face asked.

'It's Beta Gate, Sir. I'm reading a massive energy surge from the wormhole,' the young man replied in disbelief.

'That can't be right – that gateway station is due for decommissioning. You must be wrong.'

'I'm sorry, Sir, but I don't think I am.'

'Get out of the way, Boy, let me see.' The thin-faced man leaned over Peterson's console and began analysing the data being received from Beta Gate. 'Oh dear.'

'Sir?'

'Get me the chairman – it looks like a fleet from Earth.'

'But I thought the people that were left on Earth were all savages; not civilised people like–'

'Like us? No, they're not. But that doesn't alter the fact that they've somehow managed to build a fleet and traverse the wormhole,' he replied as Peterson was put on hold with the chairman's office. *'Not dismantling Olympus Shipyard was careless, but not decommissioning Beta Gate was unforgivable,'* he thought as he waited.

Dr S. Fern

OLD LIES

'Mr Chairman, I have General Moore for you. Shall I put him through?' Chairman Tabakov's secretary asked from the adjoining room, via comm-link.

The Chairman of the Government of the Russian Federation swore as he put down the report he had been reading. 'You better had, Sasha.'

'Mr Chairman, thank you for taking the time to speak to me,' a gravelly voice said from speakers inset into the chairman's desk a few seconds later.

'What can I do for you, General?' The chairman's voice was flat and toneless; relations between the Russian Federation's chairman and the chief operations officer of United Industries had always been frosty.

'It's about one of our pioneer ships, Mr Chairman; it's gone missing.'

'So you've lost contact with one of your ships. What has that got to do with the Russian Federation?'

'We lost contact with her as she was approaching Perun.'

'You mean as she was entering Russian Space, General?'

'You may have claimed the planet, Mr Chairman, but you haven't settled any of the moons,' the general snapped. Perun was the third planet in the New Earth system, and the first to be colonised when a Russian Federation Exodus Vessel landed on its surface rather than on New Earth. This had given the Russian Federation a major advantage over the other nation-alliances, and even over United

Industries in the first few decades after colonisation. The 'Federation may not have gotten around to constructing permanent settlements on any of Perun's moons yet, but they were claimed as 'Federation territories and heavily patrolled nonetheless. 'What do you know, Tabakov?' Moore snapped.

'As it happens I was made aware, just this morning, of a terrible accident involving a United Industries ship. Apparently it collided with a rogue asteroid. By the time we were able to dispatch rescue ships it was too late.' Chairman Tabakov almost managed to sound sincere.

'A rogue asteroid, is that the best you can do? An asteroid impact wouldn't have wrecked a pioneer ship.'

'I assure you, General Moore, the damage was extensive. According to the report the asteroid impacted towards the bow and tore away the starboard side of the ship.'

'I will send a vessel to recover the wreck immediately.' The venom in the C.O.O.'s voice was thick and heavy.

'I'm afraid we couldn't reach her before her drives blew. I *am* sorry, but there is nothing to recover.'

'This is outrageous! I don't believe that a mere asteroid was able to destroy a ship as large and…'

'Armed?'

'*Protected* as a pioneer ship,' Moore corrected the chairman. Officially pioneer ships were civilian vessels and therefore forbidden to mount weapons of any sort. Unofficially it was common knowledge that everyone bent the rules to some degree – United Industries not least of all. Pioneer ships were designed to be able to remain void-borne for years at a time and were consequently significant investments.

'The Russian Federation offers its sympathies but regrets that there is nothing more that it can do. Is there anything else that I can assist you with today?'

'No. That will be all.' United Industries' chief operations officer cut the link with Chairman Tabakov.

'Sasha,' the chairman spoke into the intercom, 'get me Admiral Rudnikov – I need to see him as soon as possible.'

***

'Bastard Russians!' Moore said as he punched the button that cut the link with Chairman Aleksey Tabakov. He had met many stubborn people both at United Industries and during his previous career in the Federated States Military, but no one quite like the Chairman of the Russian Federation; he would stand by official government policy no matter how patently absurd. It was simply not possible that an asteroid collision could wreck a United Industries pioneer ship. They were sturdily built and well defended – more so even than any of the specially commissioned vessels that the company had built for various clients.

Ever since the fleets had settled on New Earth, the Russian Federation had been a thorn in United Industries' side. Right from the time they had split one of their exodus vessels off from the main fleet as it approached New Earth to land on Perun, the Russians had remained doggedly self-sufficient. They had reverse engineered every U.I. component on their exodus vessels – but that wasn't all. A few decades after colonisation United Industries opened and stabilised a wormhole to The Field and began making a fortune selling mining permits. Within a few years the Russian Federation had developed their own quantum tunneller and were mining the rich asteroid field using their own wormhole, bypassing United Industries completely. United Industries or course accused the Russian Federation of stealing its intellectual property, an accusation that could neither be substantiated nor satisfactorily rebutted. This bitter dispute eventually led to hostilities and a de facto state of war had existed ever since.

As he sat behind his desk, reflecting on the many grievances he had with the Russian Federation, his hand strayed to the old Federated States service pistol that he still wore. Eventually he got up, retrieved his jacket and stormed out of his office; he didn't even acknowledge his assistant on his way out. It took Moore an hour and a half to reach his destination; the Strategic Intelligence Executive.

'Good morning, General,' the security guard in the foyer said as Moore entered.

'I need to see Ms Schmitz.'

'Please step this way, Sir.' Moore un-holstered his pistol, handed it to the guard, and stepped through the scanner. 'Thank you. This way please.'

Once his identity had been confirmed by fingerprint and retinal scans he followed the guard to a waiting room.

'I will let the director know you are here, Sir,' the guard informed him before leaving. Another guard arrived to escort him to the director's office ten minutes later. After passing through three more security check points he eventually reached the office of the director of the Strategic Intelligence Executive.

The director was a middle-aged woman with greying hair. She wore a slate grey suit, sat behind a black desk and was staring intently at the blank white screen of her desk's console.

'Please, take a seat, General, I will be with you presently,' she said. Moore sat down opposite her and waited for her to finish whatever it was she was doing. 'Please don't look at me like that,' she added a moment later. The chief operations officer averted his gaze immediately; he hadn't even realised he was staring.

A few minutes later she lifted her head to regard him for the first time since he had entered. Moore was squinting at the white console monitor. 'That won't help, General.' She pointed to her eyes. 'Polarised lenses.'

'Is that necessary? You're in one of the most secure buildings on New Earth, Director.'

'*The* most secure. It pays to be wary, General; you never know who might be in the room with you – even here. Now, how may I be of assistance?'

'We've lost a pioneer ship near Perun.'

'U32P I believe, yes I have read the report.'

'I've just been speaking to Aleksey Tabakov; he was less than helpful.'

'You suspect foul play on the part of the Russians but you have no evidence?'

'Yes. This is always the case: our ships are attacked but by the time we reach the wreck site there's nothing left to salvage. The Russians won't accept our audio logs as evidence – they insist that they could be fabrications.'

'That's an entirely fair accusation – one I would make in their position.'

'But without any hard evidence we can't take any punitive action. We don't have enough escort vessels to guard every convoy we have, never mind the lone vessels. If we had irrefutable proof that the Russians were behind these attacks then—'

'Then we could petition for help. If we could get our major clients on side we could isolate the Russian Federation and cripple it. In a few decades it would be reduced to a third-rate power. I'm afraid acquiring such proof, General, is no trifling matter. I have lost contact with three agents in the past month – I'm running out of assets. It's a painful truth that Russian security is almost as good as our own.'

'So what am I supposed to tell the chairman? We've lost another vessel, but there's nothing we can do about it?' His hand strayed to his empty pistol holster.

'A possible solution to our problem has recently presented itself. Take a look at this.' She activated a monitor on Moore's side of the desk and called up a report. The chief operations officer began to read.

'A bio-chameleonic infiltration unit; I suppose that old bastard deserves some credit – this sounds promising.' As he began reading the field-test report his eyes widened in shock. 'I met Captain Price once, Ms Schmitz, he was a man of integrity and honour – a good man. Did you have anything to do with the original assault?'

'I'm not sure I follow you, General.'

'DID YOU ARRANGE THE S.A.C. COMMANDO RAID? DID YOU KILL ALL THOSE SAILORS JUST TO FIELD-TEST ONE OF MILSEN'S NEW CREATIONS?!' Moore slammed his fist down on the screen and fixed the intelligence director with a dangerous look.

'Please, General, calm down. I'm aware that you served in the Federated States Military for many years, but you really must be more objective.' Her hand strayed under the desk. 'I'm afraid I can't discuss anything pertaining to the Alabama State that isn't in that report. Suffice to say that the field-test was a complete success. What I am about to say does not leave this room.' She waited for his nod of assent before continuing. 'We are about to deploy one of the new infiltration units directly into the Russian admiralty. Make your report regarding the loss of U32P to the Chairman as normal, but rest assured we will soon have enough information to take appropriate punitive steps.'

Moore said nothing. The knowledge that his company was behind the murder of several thousand sailors had left him feeling sick. 'I believe that will be all, General.' As he rose to leave the office door opened and a pair of security guards entered. The chief operations officer allowed himself to be escorted out. His pistol was returned to him on his way out.

He spent the return journey in deep thought and reflection. He knew that United Industries, just like everyone else, had always bent the rules to achieve their ends. What he hadn't been aware of until now was the lengths that his company was willing to go to in pursuit of profit, power and influence. If he was honest it unsettled him deeply.

Beyond Earth: New Earth

'Perhaps I'd better not be too honest with myself...'

***

Admiral Rudnikov looked up as another of his senior staff passed through the security check and was admitted into the conference room. The Russian Federation had always taken its security seriously, but recently the number of foreign agents being uncovered had fallen to almost zero. Either foreign governments had developed measures to ensure that their agents were no longer susceptible to Russian security measures, or they had stopped trying to infiltrate them entirely. Both scenarios gave the already paranoid government cause for concern. The first scenario had precipitated a step-up in internal security throughout all government facilities. The second had led the Russian intelligence service to redouble its efforts to get their own agents into the governments of every major foreign power.

'I am aware that a number of you are due to leave for Novorinya in a few hours, so I will be brief,' the admiral began, referring to the gargantuan Russian Federation space station in orbit above New Earth. 'I am sure you are all aware that a United Industries pioneer ship was lost near Perun and the accusation that —' The admiral stopped mid-sentence as the conference room door opened and the last of his senior staff entered.

'I am sorry, Admiral, I was unavoidably delayed – my aide was found dead this morning,' the middle-aged vice-admiral said as he closed the door behind him.

'Vice-admiral Gorlov, you have our condolences. Many of us knew Lieutenant Klepin – he was a good man,' the admiral said as the vice-admiral took his seat.

'I hope I haven't missed too much.'

'No, we had only just begun. I had just raised the issue of the United Industries pioneer ship that was wrecked in the vicinity of Perun.'

'Yes, I recall the incident. An asteroid collision, wasn't it?' he asked as he plugged a data stick into a terminal on the desk.

'I was about to address that very issue, Vice-admiral.' The admiral gave his subordinate a questioning look.

'I'm sorry, but with Klepin's death, I haven't had time to read all the reports; I'm just calling them up,' he replied, sweat on his brow.

'But why do you need to copy them? You have sufficient security clearance to access them on the main database.'

'I'm afraid my office has been sealed by the security services. Klepin was found in his apartment, but he worked in my office – I have to work from home for the next few days and I don't have clearance to access restricted files from there.'

'Very well,' the admiral replied as the vice-admiral began tapping away at the desk-console in front of him. 'As I was saying, the United Industries pioneer ship didn't collide with an asteroid. That's the official line, it actually hit a rotary mine.'

'Sorry, Admiral, a what?' a young counter-admiral asked.

'A *classified* weapon, Counter-admiral Pankov. As far as I understand, when they detonate, they rotate space-time around an axis creating an unstable singularity that then collapses. Suffice to say that anything caught within its blast radius is annihilated – they don't leave any detectable wreckage.'

'I hadn't even heard of their existence before now, Admiral.'

'As I said, they're a classified weapon – no one below Vice-admiral has any knowledge of their existence. You are the youngest officer to ever have formed a part of my command staff, Counter-admiral. I won't find my faith in you misplaced, will I?'

'No, Admiral – I will say nothing of this to anyone.'

'Excellent.'

'If I may ask one question, Admiral. If these weapons are classified, why are they deployed to protect Perun? Surely a conventional minefield would suffice. Why risk the existence of a classified weapon becoming common knowledge?'

'A fair question,' someone said.

'They have been deployed around Perun, Vice-admiral Ostrovsky, because they are almost impossible to detect. The objective is to make Perun a hazard to foreign navigation.'

'And so deter anyone from pressing any claim they might believe they have?' the vice-admiral replied, understanding the admiral's implication at once.

'Just so.' The admiral turned to Vice-admiral Gorlov. 'Have you finished Vice-admiral?'

'Er, yes, I've just copied the last file. I'm sorry – Klepin's death must have affected me more than I thought.'

Admiral Rudnikov was about to continue when the conference room door flew open and a man in a jet-black uniform burst in, flanked by a pair of security guards. 'What's going on?'

Colonel Nikolev, Department Sixteen.'

'How may I be of assistance, Colonel,' the admiral replied, as if having the internal security service storm his meeting was the most normal thing in the world.

'Actually, it's Vice-admiral Gorlov I have come for, or at least whoever *that* is that has been passing himself off as the vice-admiral.'

'I don't understand, is this about Lieutenant Klepin?' the vice-admiral asked, slipping the data stick into an inside pocket.

'No, it's about *you*. We discovered Vice-admiral Gorlov's body ten minutes ago – his pelvis jammed the waste disposal unit you fed him into.'

In a heartbeat the vice-admiral had leapt to his feet, vaulted onto the table and hurled himself at the colonel.

Both men crashed to the floor and before either of the security guards could react the vice-admiral had drawn his service pistol and shot the colonel in the face. By the time the guards had drawn their side arms the vice-admiral had darted through the door and was hurtling down the corridor.

***

The building's alarm was sounding before the United Industries' agent, still in the form of vice-admiral Gorlov, had reached the main foyer. He had just raced down the emergency stairwell, not wanting to risk getting cornered in a lift, and was about to make a break for the main entrance when a pair of security guards rounded a corner and ran straight in to him. He shot the first man before any of them hit the floor, but he had to bludgeon the second man to death with the butt of his pistol. He hauled both bodies into the stairwell and got to work stripping the man he had bludgeoned – his uniform might have been speckled with blood, but at least it didn't have a bloody hole shot in the centre of the chest. After tasting a little of the dead guard's blood he doubled over in pain as his chameleonic biology altered his appearance. He retrieved the data stick and a small transmitter from the vice-admiral's jacket pocket before stepping out into the corridor and walking as calmly as he could towards the main entrance. The foyer was heaving with guards who were forcing everyone through the security check points. He shouldered his way through the crowds to the front where he waited impatiently as his fingerprints and iris were scanned.

'Identity card,' a stony faced guard demanded as he attempted to step past. It should have been pinned to his left breast pocket but it wasn't – it must have torn loose in the scuffle by the stairwell. He couldn't afford to go back for it now. He began to try and bluff his way past the guard, but thought better of it and shot him instead. He just managed to dive under the portcullis-like security gate as it came crashing down and rolled clear onto the street. It was hot and humid outside and he sweated profusely as he ran. Running down one street after another he made for the docks where his one-man submersible was hopefully still concealed.

***

He might have been faster, stronger and fitter than any normal man, but the Russian Federation's renowned paranoia put them one step ahead of the fleeing United Industries operative. Several squads of military police were scouring the docks by the time he arrived and spotted him as he darted behind a stack of crates. As ion rifle fire turned his cover into blazing cinders he plugged the data stick into the transmitter and punched the emergency transmit button. A bolt of white-hot plasma finally tore through the crates and sent a shot of pain through his shoulder.

With the transmitter in one hand and a half-empty pistol in the other he made a desperate dash for the waterside. He almost made it, but was cut down by a salvo of rifle fire mere yards away. As his body burned on the dockside, a mile out to sea a United Industries submarine slipped past a patrolling frigate and out into deep water.

***

Picking up her coffee, Director Schmitz called up the recently received report. As she read the first line she put the mug down again.

'Transmission received.
'Source – UOΩ1.
'Date – 2335.06.24.1756
'Status – Partially corrupted.

Dr S. Fern

'Transmission begins:
'TOP SECRET: CLEARANCE LEVEL 10 ONLY.
'Acquisition of proprietary technologies.

'It may be reported that the Russian Federation is once again at the forefront of technological innovation. Ever since the exodus the Russian Federation has been reliant on United Industries for much of its xxx-corrupted-xxx technologies. This has led to the Federation facing crippling transit and exploration costs. Whilst other nations have been content to xxx-corrupted-xxx policy, we have not. We have worked tirelessly since colonisation to develop equivalent technologies. Indeed xxx-corrupted-xxx beyond anything United Industries currently has. We have, however, never been able to develop an equivalent to United Industries' quantum tunnellers. This was deemed unacceptable and so operation nightwing was developed and put into action.

'xxx-corrupted-xxx objective was the capture of one of United Industries' quantum tunnelling vessels. One such vessel had been docked at Gamma Gate ever since the wormhole through to The Field had been bored and stabilised. It was discovered that this vessel was due to depart Gamma Gate for Liberty One xxx-corrupted-xxx dispatched to intercept the vessel and its attendant escorts. The fleet comprised the cruiser xxx-corrupted-xxx surprise was essential. The smaller ships were armed with newly developed rotary mines. Several days after departing Gamma Gate the United Industries fleet entered the minefield that had been laid across its projected route. All of the escorting vessels were destroyed. The tunneller was immobilised xxx-corrupted-xxx before it could hit a mine. Its bridge was also shot away, preventing a distress call from being xxx-corrupted-xxx towed to Perun.

'A working prototype xxx-corrupted-xxx built and is due to put to space within the week. It is expected that the Russian Federation will have its own wormhole to The Field bored and stabilised by the end of next year. Should everything progress as expected, construction of space stations to fully anchor either end of the wormhole should be xxx-corrupted-xxx

'Colonel Lymkin.
'Department 16.'

Picking up her coffee again, the director began to read the second half of the transmission. It appeared to be the schematics for an, as yet, unknown type of deep space mine. Unfortunately the second half of the transmission was even more badly corrupted than the first half. A thought came to her and she scanned the first half of the message again. With a smile threatening to creep across her face she called Dr Milsen on a secure channel.

'Doctor, Director Schmitz here. I would like to see you at your earliest convenience; I have something here you might be able to help me with.'

'Of course, Director. I can see you this afternoon. Will that be alright?'

Yes, thank you, Doctor, that will be fine. Please bring Doctor Fairborne with you.'

'I'll see to it, Director. See you later.'

She cut the link with the technical director and drained her coffee. *'It's high time we began removing the Russian thorn from our side.'*

Dr S. Fern

Beyond Earth: New Earth

THE ORPHANS RETURN

Void Dancer exited the wormhole in the wake of the city-ship that she had been assigned to escort – Dublin. After some time the entire Settler fleet had traversed the wormhole and congregated a little way from Beta Gate. Once some semblance of order had been restored, it resumed its journey, crossing the orbit of New Jupiter and into the system's asteroid belt. Navigating this region slowed the fleet to a crawl. Whilst the smaller vessels could manoeuvre around the drifting rocks, some of which were as large as small moons, the city-ships could not. They could blast smaller objects to harmless fragments, but larger ones needed to be carefully navigated around. Eventually, however, the Settler fleet emerged from the asteroid belt and began making its way towards the orbit of Perun.

A few hours after it had emerged into open space, Void Dancer was forced to reduce speed as Dublin drifted to a halt.

'Dublin, this is Void Dancer, what's the hold-up?' Captain Krämer asked from the captain's chair.

'Void Dancer, this is Dublin, we've got a problem up ahead. Tune in to O.C.1,' the city-ship's communication's officer replied.

'Do it,' Krämer ordered. 'And while you're at it, show me what's up ahead.' The deckhand obeyed and in a few seconds Prime Minister Taylor's voice filled the bridge and a display of the space ahead of them was projected onto the main view screen.

'What do you mean *there's no available settlement sites?*' the prime minister's voice was laced heavily with anger.

'That's not good,' Krämer remarked as he saw a large number of markers, indicating ships from New Earth, drift down from the top of the view screen. It seemed as though every nation and alliance had sailed out to stop them reaching New Earth. United Industries ships were indicated alongside those of the Federated American States, the Pan Asian Alliance, the South American Coalition, the European Union, the African Union, the Kingdom of India and the Arab League.

'I mean exactly what I said, Prime Minister; there are *no available settlement sites on New Earth*. The planet's landmass is mostly comprised of island chains and archipelagos – every suitable site has been colonised. You will have to return to Earth until we can organise appropriate settlement arrangements. Your welfare is important to us, please don't mistake our inability to help at the moment for an unwillingness to help.'

'Oh I'm not mistaking either your motivations or your intentions, Captain Brunsfeld. You're seeking to placate us with promises of help and assistance so that you can destroy Beta Gate as soon as we're back on the other side. You can't possibly expect me to believe that there isn't a single settlement site left on the planet.'

'It pains me to hear you suspect me of such dishonourable intentions, Prime Minister. You have my assurance that we will do all we can to see that you are settled as rapidly and as satisfactorily as possible. I'm afraid that I cannot allow your fleet to approach any closer to New Earth, at the moment. Your presence would severely disrupt current operations, which would hamper any attempts to organise suitable settlement sites.'

'I've dealt with your type all my life, Captain – you're a liar, it's as simple as that. You have ample resources *and ample space*, but you're driven by greed. You have nothing to fear from us, Captain; we just want a share of this system's bounty and a chance to have a decent life; you have no idea what life was like after you left – it was hell. Order your ships to withdraw, Captain, we're coming through.' Krämer almost thought he could detect a hint of emotion in the prime minister's voice.

'I can't permit that, Prime Minister – under any circumstances. Please don't force me to use force; I don't want to, believe me, but I have my orders.'

'Captain, there are tens of thousands of civilians aboard each city-ship – you can't open fire and we both know it.' The prime minister's confidence had reasserted itself. Krämer watched as her city-ship, the Delhi, slowly moved towards the opposing fleet; a little green marker against a line of red.

'She's going to do it; she's actually going to do it!' Francesca exclaimed as the entire bridge crew watched the view screen with mounting tension.

'CAPTAIN, TELL YOUR SHIPS TO HOLD FIRE! I'VE GOT TENS OF THOUSANDS OF CIVILIANS ON BOARD! HOLD YOUR FIRE!' The prime minister's voice lost all of its usual confidence and authority as she pleaded with the commander of the opposing fleet.

The Delhi's marker suddenly blinked out on the view screen as the line of red ones began moving down towards the rest of the Settler fleet.

'Get us the fuck out of here, Fran,' Krämer said as the Settler fleet began turning about and scattering back towards the relative safety of the asteroid belt. Most of the smaller vessels remained with their parent city-ships and tried to protect them as best they could. The sudden appearance of the escorts' concealed weapons initially checked the advance of the New Earth fleet, but it didn't alter the fact that they were terribly out-gunned. By the time the Settlers reached the asteroid belt three more city-ships had been destroyed; Adelaide, Ho Chi Minh City and

Cape Town. The eight remaining ships split up and sought suitable places to hide.

***

The blockading fleet didn't pursue the fleeing Settlers; the larger capital ships weren't manoeuvrable enough to negotiate the asteroids and the smaller vessels were reluctant to enter without the support of their larger cousins. Void Dancer, along with most of Dublin's escorts had remained in the outer reaches of the asteroid belt whilst their ship searched for a suitable place to hide. Their role, which Krämer earnestly hoped he wouldn't be forced to perform, was to delay any pursuit for as long as possible. For three tense days the armed freighter patrolled the edge of the belt. Mercifully the only other vessels they encountered were other Settler ships. Eventually they were given a set of coordinates and called back to their parent ship.

Dublin had found herself an asteroid with a crater so deep that, not only was she not visible from orbit, but she wasn't easily detectable either. As Josh brought the freighter down into the crater it became clear that Dublin had sustained significant damage during her flight. Her bow had suffered the most; it was so heavily cratered its original shape was no longer discernible. It also looked like the port quarter had taken a significant impact.

Krämer raised the city-ship as they made their approach. 'Dublin Dock Control, this is Void Dancer, have you got a dock free?'

'Void Dancer, welcome back. Is everything quiet out there?' There was tension in the response.

'Yes, it's all quiet out here, Dock Control – we weren't followed.'

'Good.' The sound of relief was almost palpable. 'Dock two, starboard side. Bay five is free.'

'Thanks.'

Dock two was a riot of activity; nine of the ten docking bays had ships moored at them, many of them heavily damaged.

'Looks like we've taken in a number of orphans,' Josh commented as he brought Void Dancer in to dock.

'It's a fuckin' mess, Mate,' Krämer replied as the docking clamps secured the freighter with a *clunk*. 'Right, Josh, secure the ship, but don't let anyone disembark until I've figured out what's going on.' The captain got up, left the bridge and made his way to the starboard docking port.

Starboard Dock Control was heaving; a hubbub of voices filled his ears as he weaved his way towards the reporting station. The queue was three deep and the ten clerks on duty were clearly fatigued. Fifteen minutes passed, but eventually he found himself at the front of the queue.

'Yes?' a gaunt-faced clerk asked.

'I'm Captain Henry Krämer of the freighter Void Dancer; we've just docked at bay five, dock two.'

'And?'

'And I need to know whether we've been allocated quarters dockside or not.'

'Look, Captain, as well as our own ships, we've got ships from Adelaide and Ho Chi Minh City coming in. You're lucky you got a dock at all. Right now we're barely able to keep up with requests for medical assistance and emergency repair teams never mind anything else: I haven't got time to sort out quarters for you or your crew at the moment.'

'I understand, Mate, and from what I've seen you're doing a fine job. I don't need any repair teams or medical assistance – just quarters so that my crew can disembark.'

The clerk sighed and tapped away at his console. 'Okay, Deck fifty-six, section ten. Rooms forty-five to eighty-two are yours.'

'Cheers, Mate – you're a star.' The clerk barely acknowledged Henry's thanks. Before Void Dancer's captain had left the desk someone else had shouldered their way to the counter.

The rooms Krämer and his crew had been allocated were basic to say the least, but at least everyone had their own space and could take some much needed downtime. As soon as he had seen his crew to their respective quarters, Henry called up the ship's directory on his room's terminal. If Dublin had taken on ships from Adelaide it was possible that the freighter Christina was docked somewhere. After several minutes searching Henry managed to ascertain that she was at bay seven, dock eight, port-side. He set off immediately to see whether her assistant navigator and his friend, Charles Bronsen, had made it to Dublin in one piece.

It took him several hours to cross to the port-side and locate the Christina. She was in a bad way. Her stern had taken heavy damage and there were a number of deep gouges in her starboard side. He stopped a deckhand as she disembarked and asked her where they had been quartered.

'Deck forty-eight, section one thirty-two, I think,' she replied as she adjusted the burned out piece of machinery she was carrying on her shoulder.

'It took him a further forty minutes to reach deck 48, section 132. The wall terminal told him which room had been allocated to Charles. A minute later saw him standing outside a grey door with the number 480 stencilled across the top. He pressed the black button on the left hand side of the door and waited. A few seconds later Charles opened the door. The heavily tattooed assistant navigator was wearing a pair of old shorts and his trademark baseball cap. A hand-rolled cigarette hung loosely from his mouth.

'Mate! I'm so glad you're okay – I saw the Christina on my way over.'

'I was lucky, Mate. Come in?'

'Yea, alright, thanks.'

'Yea, I saw the stern; it looks bad.'

'It is – Ethan's dead, Mate, along with most of the engine room crew,' Charles replied as he pulled two cans of beer from a box under his bed.

'What happened?' Henry asked, accepting the can Charles offered him.

'I was on the bridge when they destroyed the Delhi – It was horrible. One minute she was there, the next... there was just fire, Mate, fire and explosions. Adelaide started to turn pretty much as soon as they opened fire on Delhi, but like the rest of 'em, she's a big bitch and it took her a while. By the time she was heading back to the asteroid belt they were in range. We tried to hold 'em off as best we could. At first we thought we might be able to. We hit the lead ships pretty hard – they hadn't expected us to be armed. But once the big ones closed in and began to open fire it was all over. I saw the Starlight taken out; a big fucker hit her with one shot from some massive energy cannon – one shot, Mate. They ignored us, the big ones, for the most part and headed straight for Adelaide. She'd almost made it to the asteroids when they reached her.' Charles drained his can and reached for another. 'There was nothing we could have done – not against that. We took a salvo of laser fire on the starboard beam – that wasn't too bad. It was a shot that hit the stern and blew out the engine room that fucked us up.' Charles paused and stared into the middle distance for several minutes. Henry remained silent, drinking his beer. Eventually Charles spoke again, his voice heavy with emotion. 'They never found his body, Mate – they never found any of 'em. They must be floating out there right now – that ain't right, Mate.'

'You got that right. So how'd you make it here after all that?'

'We still had thrusters. They're not designed for extended use, so they were pretty much burnt out by the time we reached you, but they got us here, so that's something. And you know what?'

'What, Mate?'

'I've still got this.' Charles pulled a metal toolbox from under his bed and held it up. 'They crippled Christina and killed my friends, but I've still got my tools; look, Mate; my gun, needles and all my inks – nothing's even damaged!' Charles managed a smile through tear-laden eyes.

'Well that's something – I've still got some places I need inked!'

'We'll have a chat, Mate; I've got a few ideas. I doubt it'll be soon, though.'

'What've you heard?'

'Just rumours really, but from what I hear, we'll be here a while.'

'Yea?'

'Yea. We haven't got the fire-power to fight our way to New Earth and we're not going back through the wormhole—'

'Too fuckin' right.'

'Right, and we're pretty well hidden in the asteroid belt. So there's rumours that, Dublin at least, is planning on staying right here. There's enough ice in the surrounding asteroids to supply us with water, air and fuel indefinitely. Then there's the iron ore and everything else that can be mined.'

'So you're saying we're settling here, in the arse-crack of an asteroid?'

'It could be worse, Mate.'

'Really?!'

'The Delhi was carrying the prime minister *and* her entire government...'

'So right now there's no one in charge?'

'Nope, and from what I've heard there's been no word from any of the other city-ships – they're all keeping quiet in case they're discovered.'

'So who's in charge?'

'Dubin's captain's calling the shots at the moment.'

'But he's not got enough crew to run the entire place, surely?'

'Nope.'

'So there's *actually* no one in charge?'

'Nope. There's no one telling you what to do or where to go – we're free to do what we like, Mate.'

'Su-fucking-perb – that's the first bit of good news I've heard in a long time.'

'You know what I'd do, if I were you?'

'Get pissed?'

'Before that. Head up to the command deck; my captain's gone up there to see what work they've got going while the repairs are being made.'

'*Work?*'

'There might be no one in charge now, Mate, but we've still got to earn a living.'

'Fair point.'

'I'd head up pretty soon – there's a lot of work going but a lot of it'll be mining work and you don't want to spend months on end baby-sitting a mining rig.'

'No, Mate, I don't.' Henry drained his can. 'Thanks for the beer. I think I'll head over now and see if I can pick up a decent job. You about for a few beers later?'

'I might be needed on Christina, but if not I'll let you know. What cabin are you in?'

'Deck fifty-six, section ten, room forty-five.'

'Cool; I'll let you know.'

'Alright, Mate – see you later.' Henry left Charles' cabin as his friend re-lit his cigarette and began staring into the middle distance again. Ethan's death had clearly hit him harder than he had admitted.

As he made his way to Dublin's command deck Henry began to consider the implications of a life with no government, no authority he *had* to obey, and the fact that he was now entirely responsible for his own future. He could have anything he wanted; he had a ship and a crew – *anything*.

The command deck was busy – it always was. Eventually he found his way to the assignments office where he found he wasn't the only captain who was hoping to secure one of the better jobs. After around a quarter of an hour one of the terminals became free and he keyed in his identification code. A list of available assignments was displayed and the freighter captain read through each of them in turn. Quite a few were baby-sitting jobs.

'I ain't playing nanny to a mining rig for two months,' he grumbled as he scrolled down the list. He smiled as he reached the convoy assignments. 'An ore-harvest; that'll do.'

'Rock picking they mean,' a voice from behind him said.

Henry turned and came knee-to-face with a nervous looking midget. 'Yea, but at least I won't be hanging around for a couple of months for a mining rig to set up before I can fill my hold.'

'Fair point,' the midget replied, his breathing rapid. 'I'm looking for something similar. I'm Thomas Roberts, captain of the Starfish.'

'Henry Krämer, captain of the Void Dancer. Are you alright? You don't look well.'

'I'll be alright – I don't like crowds, that's all,' Thomas replied, idly running his right hand over the scarred remains of his left hand.

'Fair enough, Mate – don't let me keep you. Good luck.'

'Thanks, you too,' Thomas replied as he strode up to the terminal and rapidly keyed in his identification code.

***

The convoy, OH04, departed two days later and headed into the asteroid belt in search of ore-rich asteroids to break up and return to the processing plants back at Dublin. Usually Henry would give his crew a week's shore leave between jobs, but in this case it was obvious that they were all ready to leave; Dublin had become far too crowded since taking on most of the surviving ships that had sailed with Adelaide.

Convoy OH04 consisted of two large ships equipped with mass drivers and remotely operated harvest drones. These ships would break up any asteroids that were too large to be transported directly into the holds of the convoy's ten freighters.

'So, what're we getting for this run, Captain?' Lieutenant Vega asked as the convoy began searching for asteroids rich in metal ores.

'It's a flat rate, Mate.'

'What?'

'Yea, that's all that was on offer. At least it's something though.'

'I suppose so – I just prefer it when there's an opportunity to make a bit more than just basic rate.'

'I know, Mate – we all feel the same, but at the moment it's either this or baby-sitting mining rigs.'

'I'm not complaining, Captain—'

'You were – but that's okay – this is a crap job. Better ones'll come along and I'll do whatever it takes to get them – trust me.'

'Captain?'

'What is it, Sylv?'

'We're next up, Captain.'

'Alright, secure internal hold hatches and prepare to open the outer doors.'

'Internal hatches secured, Captain, preparing to…'

'What is it, Sylv?'

'It's the convoy, Captain, the ships in front are changing course; they're heading for the far side of that massive asteroid off the starboard bow.'

'Why?'

'I don't—'

'Captain?'

'What is it, Adolfo?'

'Two ships have just come within range of our long-range scanners.'

'What are they?'

'I'm not sure, Captain, not from this range. They're broadcasting African Union call-signs.'

'So they're not Settlers. Sylv, can you get us closer without being spotted?'

'Probably, Captain, but why would we want to? The rest of the convoy's heading in the other direction.'

'We're on a flat rate job, right?'

'Yea, so?'

'Just get us closer, Sylv.'

'You're the boss, Cap,' the second mate replied as she plotted a new course through the asteroids.

For the next hour Void Dancer slipped between asteroids, stalking the two African Union vessels that had panicked the Settler convoy. Eventually Sylvia edged the freighter from behind an asteroid and initiated a full scan of the two African vessels. One was a large bulk carrier, the Fola Okonjo, the other was the Lusaka, a frigate class escort.

'Have they detected us yet, Sylv?'

'I don't think so, Cap.'

'What's the frigate packing?'

'It looks like a pair of laser batteries, Cap. What're you thinking?'

'Adolfo, could you hit that frigate from here?'

'Yes, Captain, I could,' the lieutenant replied after a pause.

'In that case I think it's time to earn a little bit more than the flat rate!'

'Oh shit, Cap, are you planning on doing what I think you are?' Sylvia asked.

'If you're thinking that I'm about to order Adolfo to blow the shit out of that frigate and then seize the carrier, you're absolutely right.'

'Do you want me to plot a firing solution, Captain?'
'Yes, ideally before they spot us.'
'Solution plotted, Captain.'
'Right, Sylv, get ready to jump that carrier.'
'Righto, Cap'.'
'FIRE!'

A second after later Void Dancer's twin rail cannons opened fire. Lusaka's dispersion fields flashed briefly before collapsing. She began to turn but a second later a second salvo tore her in half. Her back broken, she voided and died.

'NOW, SYLV, NOW!' Void Dancer shot out into open space and came to a halt in front of the Fola Okonjo.

'Sylv, raise the captain.'

'This is Captain Magoro of the bulk carrier Fola Okonjo to the hostile vessel off our bow, identify yourself.'

'Captain Magoro, this is Captain Krämer of the Void Dancer. Might I ask what cargo you're carrying?'

'Just refined ores; iron, nickel and cobalt. Why did you attack the Lusaka? That is an act of war, Captain.'

'Maybe if I was an alliance or Federation vessel or something, but I'm not, Mate, so it can't be *an act of war*, can it?'

'Then you're committing piracy, Captain; the Union will hear of this, you can be sure of that.'

Maybe they will, but that's not much help now, is it?'

'Speak plainly, Captain, what do you want?'

'Your cargo. Hand it over and I'll let you get on your way.'

'I'll need some time to prepare the hold…and organise the unloading…'

'Captain, he's playing us. He's just sent a distress call,' Sylvia interrupted.

'Captain Magoro, stop fuckin' about and open your holds; I don't want to hurt anyone.'

'By now, Captain, other African Union ships are on their way to our aid. There's still time for your to leave – no one needs to get hurt here.'

'You silly bastard, I said I didn't *want* to hurt anyone, but I didn't say I wouldn't.' Henry cut the link to the Fola Okonjo. Adolfo, target their bridge.'

'Aye, Captain.' Void Dancer's three dorsal turrets turned and locked on to the bulk carrier's bridge. A second later they opened fire.

'How many void-loaders have we got, Sylv?'

'Three, Captain.'

'Right, get them over there and begin transferring the cargo. I want to be out of here well before anyone else turns up.

'Righto, Cap.'

It took several hours to transfer the entirety of the Fola Okonjo's cargo.

'Captain, I'm picking up three vessels on the long-range scanners,' Sylvia said as one of the remotely operated void-loaders entered the aft hold.

'How much longer until we've loaded everything?'

'That's the last load we can take, Captain. There's still some iron ore left, but we're full.'

'Right, then get us the hell out of here.'

As the cargo hold doors closed Void Dancer turned and headed back through the asteroids towards Dublin where Henry hoped to be able to sell his haul for far more than the flat rate he had originally signed on for.

'He was right, you know, Cap,' Sylvia said as they approached the asteroid in which Dublin was hidden.

'What, Captain Magoro?'

'Yea; we're not registered with any nation, alliance, or anything, so we are *actually* pirates.'

'What's your point, Sylv? D'you want me to start wearing a stupid hat or something?'

'No, Cap, I just thought I'd say. You've not got a problem, have you, Adolfo?'

'No, Sylvia – It looks like it pays better than convoy duty!'

'That it does...' Henry agreed as Void Dancer came in to dock.

Dr S. Fern

VANGUARD

Eight light years from New Earth the five planets of the Anderson System orbit their red giant star, officially designated A5613-β. This system was the first to be surveyed by United Industries once it had established itself in the New Earth system. Once a wormhole had been bored and stabilised with jump gates, exploration permits were sold to whoever could afford the exorbitant prices being charged.

Tanxing, a small civilian outpost administered by the Pan Asian Alliance, nestled in a crater on the surface of A5613-β-4-3, the third moon of the fourth planet of the Anderson System.

'Report,' Magistrate Chén demanded as he entered the main operations centre.

'All extractors are operating at maximum capacity, Sir, except Mr Wu's – they've reported a problem with their primary drive system and have had to shut it down for repairs,' a clerk replied from one of the three-dozen terminals that filled the room.

'We can't afford any delays; we have a quota to reach before the convoy arrives in three weeks.'

'But, Sir, Mr Wu needs to shut down his reactor in order to repair it.'

'Then I suggest you order the other reactors run beyond their rated maximums, Mr Lung – these systems have extra capacity built in for a reason,' the magistrate stated before continuing his tour of the operations centre.

'Ms Tam, how are the water purifiers?'

'They're operating at capacity, Magistrate; we will meet our quota of fuel-grade water by the time the convoy arrives.'

'Good, that is what I like to hear. Mr Kato,' the magistrate continued, turning to the outpost's chief meteorologist, 'I hope you're going to tell me that everything is quiet outside.'

'Actually, Magistrate, I have been picking up some odd interference. I hadn't reported it before because I didn't know what to report it as.'

'But you do now, I hope.'

'Yes, Sir, I think so. It looks like we've got an incoming meteor shower.'

'A meteor shower, here?'

'It's unusual, I know, but that's what it looks like.'

'You're sure?'

The meteorologist paused to recheck his instruments before replying. 'Yes, Sir, I'm sure – it should reach us in about six hours.'

'Very well, order the dispersion field raised and send out the usual warnings,' the magistrate said before completing his inspection. Once he was satisfied that everything was operating as efficiently as it could, he left the outpost's nerve centre and made his way to his quarters.

Once inside the small, sparsely furnished set of rooms he shut the door, unbuttoned his deep blue jacket, and slumped down into the chair behind his desk. He took one look at the pile of production reports, colony status dispatches and other extraneous official communiques, sighed deeply, and pulled a small ceramic bottle and a cup from the bottom drawer of his desk. He poured himself a measure of Baijiu, knocked back the strong liquor in a single draught and poured himself another.

'Volunteer for the frontier – Serve yourself and the Alliance!' the posters had said.

Beyond Earth: New Earth

'Sure; I was fast-tracked to 'magistrate', but what now?' he looked across the room at a copy of the poster that had lured him out to this godforsaken patch of space. 'Serve yourself!' he laughed, mocking himself as much as the propaganda on the far wall. 'Well, it's not quite the type of *service* I had in mind, but I'll take all I can get out here…' he trailed off into a self-pitying monologue as he poured another cup of Baijiu.

He woke suddenly to the sound of the colony-wide alarm. His throat was dry, his neck ached and his body was stiff from where he had passed out in his chair. The empty spirit bottle lay on its side, almost accusingly, on the desk in front of him. Cursing, he dashed it to the floor as he pulled himself upright.

'What's happening?' he asked.

No reply.

This time he jabbed the correct button on his desk. 'What's happening?'

'It's the field, Sir – it's failed!'

'What do you mean? What about the reserve capacitors?'

'They've all blown, Sir!'

'I thought it was just a meteor shower?'

'It's more like a storm, Sir – we're receiving damage reports across the whole colony.'

'I'll be right there.' After breaking the link, Chén pulled his jacket on and made his way back to the operations centre.

It was chaos; a dozen sirens were sounding and twice as many warning lights were blinking across the centre's consoles. Assaulted by the cacophony of sound and light, he stopped fumbling with the buttons of his jacket, placed his hands across his forehead and began massaging his temples.

'Sir!' a dozen voices said at once.

'Turn those sirens off – I can't hear myself think!'

'But, Sir!' someone remonstrated.

Dr S. Fern

'TURN THE DAMNED ALARMS OFF!'

One by one the alarms were silenced.

'Right, one at a time, what's happening?'

'We've lost the colony shield, Sir – the meteors knocked it out,' someone began.

'We're taking damage across the whole site,' someone else added.

'Sir, are –'

'Stop,' the magistrate interrupted. 'What damage have we suffered so far?'

'A couple of habitation domes have been ruptured, but we've only lost a few zones. The power station took a hit but shut itself down. Three of the extractors have been destroyed and one of the water purifiers has taken some damage.'

'How long before we can get repair crews out to the damaged areas?'

'Sir, the storm's not over – I'm still receiving impact reports – I'm not—' The operations centre was suddenly cast into pitch darkness.

'What—'

'The reserve generator's just shut down, Sir,' someone said.

'Well get it back on then!'

'It's not that simple, Sir – it's at the other end of the complex. A repair crew should be being dispatched now; they'll get it working again soon.' Whoever it was didn't sound at all confident.

'Well I suggest you head over there and find out *exactly* how long it's going to take!' the magistrate snapped.

'But I can't—' Slowly several lambent green lights began to glow – the emergency lights had come on.

'Okay, I won't be long.'

'Wait, take a radio too – the complex's comm-links don't have a dedicated power supply,' someone, possibly Mr Kato, suggested

'Thanks.'

The wait was interminable. Slowly, carefully, men and women found each other and began huddling together in small groups. No one found Magistrate Chén who had backed into a corner and screwed his eyes tightly shut.

'Magistrate? Anyone? It's Mr Ho; I've reached the reserve generator, well, as close as I can get,' the radio crackled.

'Mr Ho, this is Mr Kato. Are you okay?'

'Yes, I'm fine. Wait, I can see movement inside the reserve generator room, hold on…'

'What is it? Are the repair crew already there?'

'What the… It's not the repair crew, Mr Kato; I don't know what it is – I can't see it clearly…'

'Describe what you can see?'

I can see the reserve generator – it's clearly damaged. It looks like a piece of meteorite has embedded itself in it but it's…'

'It's what, Mr Ho? What can you see?'

'It looks like… It can't be…'

'WHAT?!'

'It looks like a large arm or, tentacle or, something, has burst through the wall and attached itself to the generator.'

'Are you—'

'The room's coming apart, Mr Kato – I can see cracks appearing in the wall. Wait, what… AAARRGGGHHH!!!!'

'Mr Ho? MR HO?!'

Silence.

'What now?' someone asked.

'The emergency transmitter has its own power supply. We must call for help and then make our way to one of the undamaged complexes,' Mr Kato suggested after a pause that told all that needed to be told of the magistrate's state of mind. 'Ms Ts'ao, are you here?'

'Yes,' a small, weak voice replied.

'Please get the transmitter working. The rest of us, why don't we gather together by the door, ready to get to the airlock once Ms Ts'ao has finished?' Subdued mutters of agreement answered Mr Kato's suggestion.

Several minutes passed in muted silence as the young communications officer set up the emergency transmitter.

'Right, it's set up to broadcast on all major—'

B*oom!*

Several cracks began to form in the centre's reinforced wall, cracks that rapidly began to lengthen.

'Get out! NOW!' Mr Kato shouted as he barrelled past the magistrate and pulled the door open. In the gloom the entire compliment of the operations centre stumbled out and down the corridor in blind panic.

Magistrate Chén lost his way and became separated from his staff. He stumbled for several minutes along corridor after corridor until he found himself at his quarters. Alone, despairing, and entirely without the first idea what he should do, he collapsed into his desk chair as he had so many nights before. This time, however, he sat down in almost complete darkness; a single green emergency strip provided the only illumination. Sobbing and at his wit's end, he reached into the bottom drawer of his desk and fumbled for the other bottle of Baijiu.

***

Captain Yo commanded the small task force that was cruising at top speed towards Epsilon Gate; the jump gate that led to the outer reaches of the Anderson System. Comprised of the rescue vessel Zhoushi, a squadron of frigates and Captain Yo's own command, the light cruiser Xutong, the task force wasn't large, but it was fast – and that was what mattered. She had left Xujing, the vast Pan Asian Alliance naval base on New Earth's first moon, a little over five hours after the distress call had been received. The plea for help had been received by Anderson One, the gateway station that stabilised the Anderson System end of the wormhole, and promptly relayed through to Epsilon Gate. There had, however, been a delay of almost thirteen hours between its reception at the United Industries gate and it being passed on to the communications nexus at Xujing.

Admiral Wei had been furious when he learned that the message was thirteen hours old. 'How can they possibly delay passing on a message like this?' he had bellowed at his senior communications officer.

'Apparently it had something to do with unpaid transmission fees, Sir,' the officer had replied.

'Unpaid fees? We pay all our fees to those leeches, every month!'

'Apparently fees relating to the Anderson System are settled by a different department, Sir; it took our treasury some time to reach the correct one.'

'And all this time we have settlers in need of help – help we can't send because we have *no idea* that it needs to be sent!' The admiral had been fuming by this point. 'Curse their bureaucracy!'

'Sir,' someone interrupted the admiral's rant.

'What is it, Ensign Hao?'

'Sir, I've called up today's status reports. There are currently six search and rescue ships in dock; one of them, the Zhoushi, could be made ready to leave in a few hours.'

'Good. Thank you, Ensign. What other vessels can be ready in the same time period?'

'Well, the battlesh—'

'Nothing larger than a cruiser, Ensign – speed is of the utmost importance.'

'Sorry, Sir... erm... the only capital ship that can be ready in time is a light cruiser; the Xutong. There's also a squadron of type 78Y frigates that can put to space too. Everything else is either too slow, re-fitting, or has just returned from patrol and needs to re-supply.'

'Very well, it's not ideal but it will have to do. Contact the Xutong, the Zhoushi and the frigates and tell their commanders to be prepared to put to space.'

Dr S. Fern

***

We have made good time, Captain,' Commander Takada said as the Xutong approached Epsilon Gate.

'Yes, Commander, we have. What is the transit time through the wormhole?'

'Fifteen minutes, Captain. From there is should take us no more than eight hours to reach Tanxing.' The captain appeared not to have heard his second-in-command. 'Sir?'

'Yes, Commander, I heard you,' she said before turning to her communications officer. 'Ensign Chang, why haven't we been given clearance by Epsilon Station yet?'

'Our request for transit is queued, Captain.'

'What do you mean *queued*?'

'I don't know, Captain, that's all I've been told.'

'You are relieved, Ensign,' she said between gritted teeth as she strode over to the communications station. Jabbing the console in frustration she opened a link with the station's transit centre. 'Epsilon Station, this is Captain Yo of the P.A.A. cruiser Xutong, why haven't we been given clearance to enter the wormhole yet? We are on an urgent rescue mission.'

'Captain Yo, this is Mr Müller at Epsilon Station transit control. I'm sorry for the delay, we are having some difficulty calling up your permits. It would seem as though your government submitted them to the wrong department; it might take some time to call them up—'

'I don't *have* time, Mr Müller – my vessels *must* be allowed to transit as soon as possible.'

'I'm afraid it's not as simple as that, Captain. You must have the correct documentation—'

'To Hell with the documentation – people's lives are at stake you snivelling bureaucrat!'

'Captain, please, I'm just trying to do my job. I can sell you an emergency permit. That will authorise your vessels for a single passage through the wormhole. I can send you the application if—' Captain Yo punched the console, breaking the link.

'Commander Takada, arm both the dorsal and ventral rail cannon batteries.

'Captain? Nobody starts a fight with a space station it would be—'

'I am well aware what it would be, Commander. Target the main operations deck, and if you can, zero in on the transit control centre.'

'Aye aye, Captain,' the commander replied with a sly grin before turning to one of the bridge crew. 'Lieutenant-commander Song, arm both rail cannon batteries and target Epsilon Station – lock on to the transit control centre.'

'Aye, aye, Sir.'

A few seconds later Ensign Chang received an incoming transmission. 'Captain Yo, this is Mr Müller – I have just managed to retrieve your transit permit – you are clear to enter the wormhole.' Mr Müller sounded more than a little panicked. A wicked grin threatened to break the captain's stony countenance.

'Take us in, Commander,' she said, not bothering to acknowledge the transit manager.

***

A little more than eight hours after entering the wormhole Captain Yo's task force entered orbit around the third moon of the fourth planet of the Anderson System.

'Ensign Chang, raise Tanxing,' the captain ordered.

'There's no response, Sir,' the ensign replied.

'But the emergency signal is still broadcasting?'

'Yes, Captain, but it's probably an automated broadcast.'

'Ensign Kondo, scan the complex.'

'I'm not detecting any major energy readings, Captain. There's no significant temperature differential either – it looks like most of the structures took major damage in the meteor storm... just a minute, that's odd...'

'What is it, Ensign?'

'It looks like the complex took much more damage than the surrounding landscape.'

'That's hardly surprising; if their field failed, they'd be bound to take more damage.'

'No, Commander, that's not what I mean; it looks like the complex took more hits than the surrounding landscape, a *lot* more. Look.' The ensign projected the analysis currently on his monitor up onto one of the bridge's main view screens. The analysis showed the Tanxing complex as well as the surrounding ten miles of lunar landscape.

'Highlight all new impacts, Ensign.' Several hundred impact craters were suddenly highlighted on the main projection. Most of them overlaid the civilian complex.

'This is disturbing...' Captain Yo said as she slowly paced the bridge. 'Contact the Zhoushi and tell her to send rescue parties to the surface immediately.' She paused and then added, 'Send a platoon of marines down with them.'

'Captain, I'm picking up a strange contact entering the system on the long-range scanners.' Commander Takada looked up from where he was dispatching the rescue parties and their marine escorts.

Captain Yo stopped pacing the bridge. 'Who is it?'

'I'm not sure, Captain, I don't recognise the energy signature or the vessel configuration – although from this distance the readings are sketchy.'

'Commander, how long until all the landing parties are away?'

'A few minutes, Captain.'

'Good. I want to intercept that vessel – I don't care who it is, I don't want them anywhere near this settlement.'

'Aye, aye, Captain. Helmsman, plot an intercept course and transmit it to the frigates.'

'Aye, aye, Sir.'

'Wait, I don't want to leave the Zhoushi without an escort,' the captain interrupted. 'Tell the Sandao to remain behind with the Zhoushi – the other three can accompany us.'

'Aye, aye, Sir.'

Once the captain's orders had been transmitted, the helmsman broke Xutong's orbit around the moon and directed her towards the mysterious long-range contact.

***

'First squad, secure a perimeter around the shuttles, squads two and three, with me,' Lieutenant Kimura ordered as she launched herself down the shuttle's assault ramp. She'd had enough experience in low gravity environments to ensure that her steps weren't the long, slow glides of a new recruit. Her entire platoon were veterans of the Sulphur War; a short but brutal war between the Pan Asian Alliance and the Federated American States that was fought over the sulphur lakes of New Io – the first planet in the New Earth system. The second and third squads of the lieutenant's platoon followed her as she rapidly crossed the open ground between the shuttles and the perimeter of the Tanxing complex. Three rescue parties, all in white void suits, followed in the marines' wake. These men and women hadn't had much experience in low gravity and so followed slowly.

'Squad two; standard search pattern, squad three; with me – we're heading for the operations centre.' The lieutenant didn't need to check her helmet's internal display to check whether her orders were being followed – she knew and trusted her marines implicitly.

'Lieutenant, some thing's not right – these meteor craters, they're... well, Lieutenant, they're just wrong – I don't like it.'

'What are you seeing, Sergeant?' she asked as she led her accompanying squad into the administration complex.

'There are meteorites in these craters, Lieutenant.
'Where are you?'
'We're currently halfway between the main administration complex and the habitation domes.'
'Are you sure they're meteorites? Could they be unexploded ordinance? The administration complex has sustained a lot of damage – what we're seeing wasn't caused by a meteor storm.' She paused whilst the marine on point ahead of her negotiated a pile of masonry that almost blocked the passageway.
'I don't know, sir – it's difficult to see from here. Permission to enter the crater?'
'Granted, proceed with caution, Sergeant.' After negotiating more partially blocked passageways, the lieutenant and her squad finally reached the operations centre. She didn't need to issue any orders; her soldiers knew their jobs.
'Main power's out, Lieutenant, as is the backup; we're not going to get any of the complex's systems up without the mobile generator from the shuttle.'
'Thank you, Zhou. Help Tanaka set up the command post.'
'Aye, Sir.'
'Lieutenant, this is Sergeant Lee, I've descended into one of the craters. It's definitely a meteorite, Lieutenant. It's odd, though.'
'How so?'
'Well, it's like it's… well, it's like it's latched onto the surface of the moon, Lieutenant…'
'Make sense, Marine; what exactly are you seeing?'
'Well, it definitely impacted at speed, Lieutenant; the impacting face has squashed flat against the surface of the moon – I guess it just *looks* like it's latching on to it, Sir. It's the fallout that's making the men nervous.'
'*Fallout?*'
'Yes, Sir. There are four rays of ejecta… but they look like arms, Sir…'

'Pull yourself together, Sergeant; what you're seeing is probably the result of the impact of an object with a core of unusually high density surrounded by an outer shell of a much lower density material.'

'No, Sir, no it's not…'

'What do you mean, *it's not*?'

'It's not, Sir, because it's moving, it's AAARRRGGHHH!!!!'

'Sergeant?'

Silence.

'SERGEANT!'

'Lieutenant, this is Private Lopez – it's eating him, Sir!' Lieutenant Kimura winced as laser rifle fire filled her headset.

'Private Lopez, come in!'

'Anyone from squad two, respond!'

'Sir, this is Corporal Ho; it's alive, Lieutenant – the meteorite – it's just come alive!'

'What do you mean *it came alive*, Corporal?'

'I mean it pulled itself out of the ground and attacked us with its tentacle-arm things – they've got fucking great mouths on the end of them, Sir – and we can't bring it down!' Again the lieutenant's headset was filled with the sound of desperate rifle fire.

'Tanaka, where's my command post?'

'It's just coming on-line, Lieutenant.'

'Good, show me second squad,' she snapped as she strode across the room, stepping over rubble that had once been the far wall.

'I'm only picking up signals from three, wait, no, two of the squad, Sir; I think there's something wrong with the equipment…'

'There's nothing wrong with the equipment, Tanaka. Set up Broad Report – include everyone; the rescue teams, the fleet, everyone.'

'What's happening, Sir?'

'I don't know. All I know is that we've just lost most of second squad.' It wasn't standard procedure for an officer to take lower ranks into confidence, but Lieutenant Kimura and her platoon weren't a standard platoon – they'd been through so much together that they were more a family than a military unit.

'Sir, I've set up the communications link. What are your orders?' There was an uncertainty in the voice of the marine who was usually one of the most dependable of the lieutenant's platoon.

She didn't answer at once. 'Lieutenant Kimura to all rescue teams, report.'

'This is team three, we haven't found anyone yet, Sir.'

'Team one reporting – we haven't found anyone either.'

'Team four – nothing either.'

'Team two reporting. We haven't found anyone either – no casualties, no bodies – nothing, Lieutenant…'

'This is Lieutenant Kimura to all teams; fall back to the shuttles. I repeat fall back to the shuttles.' The lieutenant cut the link and turned to her squad. 'This is no longer a rescue mission.'

***

The Xutong sped silently though the void, flanked by her three escorting frigates, towards the fifth and last planet in the Anderson System.

'Ensign Kondo, time to intercept?'

'Fifteen minutes, at present speed, Captain.'

'Time until close-range scanners come into range?'

'Ten minutes, Captain.'

'Helmsman, slow to half speed in ten minutes; I want as much information as possible before we engage.'

'Aye, aye, Sir.'

The intervening five minutes passed in silence.

'Contact within range of high-resolution scanners, Captain.'

'On screen.'

The central of the bridge's view screens projected a view directly ahead of the cruiser. The small vessel in the centre of the screen slowly grew in size until it filled it. It was tear-drop shaped, trailed tendrils, and delicate frills ran the length of it. It was difficult to determine the vessel's colour from the view on the bridge monitor; it could have been a blue-green.

'What the hell is *that*, Commander?'

'It's not a configuration I'm familiar with, Captain. My only guess is that it's some new U.I. vessel.'

It's possible—'

'I'm receiving a transmission, Captain, audio only.'

'Let's hear it.'

'We are in advance. Across void. Transit.'

'What's wrong with our translators, Ensign Chang?'

'Nothing, Captain; they're working... as far as I can tell.'

'Spread. Barren from. To go. Resources to be rich.'

A heavy silence fell across the bridge of the Xutong as the terrible truth slowly sank in.

'Captain, that vessel...'

'Is not human. Thank you, Commander; that much is clear. Suggestions?'

'Raise fields and power weapons.'

'That would be the logical option, Commander, I agree, but we find ourselves in an entirely novel situation. This race might not be hostile... it could turn out to be a great ally to the 'Alliance. Do not raise shields or arms weapons yet.'

'Aye, Sir.' The Commander did not sound as certain as his captain.

'Alien vessel, we are having trouble understanding you. Could you provide a visual link?'

There was a delay of some minutes before the reply came through. 'Visual link is equals to see.'

'Yes, to see you would help us,' the captain replied, trying to keep her sentences as simple as possible.

Several minutes passed in tense silence on the bridge until Ensign Chang received another transmission from the alien vessel. 'I'm receiving another transmission, Captain; audio-visual this time.'

'On screen.'

'The image on bridge's main view screen was initially obscured by what appeared to be steam or mist. Slowly the view cleared enough for the bridge crew to make out a shadowy shape in the background. Most of the figure's features were obscured but it was clearly taller than it was broad and appeared to have numerous appendages. A dark shape surrounded it; either a shadow cast by some architecture of the bridge that was out of shot, or a part of the creature's anatomy.

'How is it that you speak our language?' Captain Yo asked, this time in Mandarin instead of English.

'Translator we to own. To show, to put at ease, your mind?'

'Yes, please. I would like to see how you are able to understand us,' the captain replied, this time in Cantonese. The view on the screen slowly panned down until what appeared to be a large machine came into view. As the mist cleared it became clear that the machine was at least as much organic as it was mechanical. It wasn't this that caused the breaths of the entire bridge crew to catch in their throats, however, rather, it was the two men and one woman who were surgically attached to it that did. Several pipes and cables ran into the first man's throat; his eyes had been sewn shut and his ears sealed. Cables ran into the second man's ears; his eyes and mouth had been sewn shut. The woman had a pair of cables running into her eye sockets; her mouth had been sewn shut and her ears had been sealed.

'What have you done?' The captain failed to disguise her disgust.

'Necessary to communicate. Many individuals you have. Low value three.'

'They… You…' Captain Yo was unable to articulate the rage that had erupted inside her. 'Raise fields and arm weapons,' she snapped.

'Aye, Sir,' Commander Takada replied once he had torn his gaze from the horror on the view screen.

'Cut the link, Ensign,' the captain said, turning her back on the screen.

'Weapons ready, Captain.'

'Fire!'

The Xutong's field's dropped for a split second to allow the dorsal and ventral rail cannon batteries to open fire. The alien vessel was raked by high velocity solid projectiles. Bright flashes indicated the points of impact: the alien vessel was clearly projecting some kind of energy field. By the time the rail cannon ordinance impacted the vessel's hull it barely marked its surface. A moment after the Xutong opened fire, its escorting frigates moved to flank the alien vessel and rake it with laser fire. A split second after the Xutong opened fire, the alien vessel, seemingly ignoring the flanking frigates, launched itself at the light cruiser.

'HELMSMAN, EVADE!' the captain shouted as the central view screen was filled with a view of the alien vessel's underside. The Xutong might have been a light cruiser and so capable of tighter manoeuvres than a fully fledged capital ship, but she was still no match for the alien. She shuddered as the closing vessel slammed its underside into her port beam.

'Report!'

'Hull breaches reported on decks three through ten, Captain.'

'Secu—'

'Enemy contacts reported on decks four, six, eight and nine, Captain!' another bridge officer announced, cutting the captain off mid-sentence.

Dr S. Fern

'Secure decks three through ten, priority four through nine!'

'Aye, aye, Sir!'

Before long running battles were erupting along most of Xutong's midsection; squads of marines fought hopeless rearguard actions against void-toughened tendrils. Laser carbines cut insignificant grooves in semi-metal vines whilst lamprey-like mouths consumed sailors whole. Meanwhile the three flanking frigates poured salvo after salvo of laser fire onto the alien ship to no avail; its field dispersed the incoming fire to the point of insignificance. Gaining confidence from the lack of return fire, Xutong's frigates closed to point blank range at which point the alien vessel's trailing tendrils lashed out and ensnared the escorts.

'Damage report!' Captain Yo demanded before being thrown to the deck as the Xutong was rocked violently to starboard.

'I've lost contact with, and have void reports for, every deck amidships, Captain.'

'Status of the enemy?'

'Apparently undamaged, Captain. It appears to have ensnared the frigates as well.' Commander Takada's usually cool exterior was beginning to show signs of cracking.

'Is there nothing we can do?!'

'Everything we have tried has failed, Captain! The enemy is too close for any of our weapons systems to open fire.'

'Captain, we have to aband—' Commander Takada was cut off mid-sentence as the blast door leading onto the bridge disintegrated. A maw the size of the passageway came through and launched itself at the secondary operations station; the largest concentration of machinery on the bridge.

Cursing in every language she knew, Captain Yo drew her side arm and emptied all of her three clips into the tentacle-arm that was reducing the operations station to scrap metal.

In little more than a minute the secondary ops position had been entirely consumed. The tentacle-arm pulled itself from the ruin, its maw quivering as if it were tasting the air. It turned to face Captain Yo, standing on the command bridge.

She had always considered her officer's sword a purely ceremonial accoutrement, but now, faced with the loss of her first capital command, it had a greater value. Given the damage her vessel had already sustained, and the damage it was continuing to sustain, she knew the Xutong was lost. She knew her crew were as good as dead, and she knew that there was nothing she could do about it. Calmly, she drew he sword, pushed her shoulders back, her chest out, and prepared to meet death.

Death, when it came was little more than sharp pain followed by black oblivion.

***

A slight flicker on the terminator of the fourth planet of the Anderson System threatened to give away a vessel on silent running. Fortunately no one was paying attention; the P.A.A. rescue vessel was busy docking a small flight of shuttles whilst its erstwhile guardian was busy being ravaged by the unstoppable alien. As the alien vessel passed the crippled hulk of the frigate to its trailing appendages it accelerated towards the fleeing rescue vessel.

From the cover of the planet's night-side a small cutter, bearing the markings of United Industries, slipped into the void, stalking the alien…

Dr S. Fern

POSTEHUMAN

The one-man scout craft slid silently through the void, from the illumination of its parent ship's search lights into the pitch darkness of the abandoned shipyard.

'Delphine, this is scout three, I've just entered one of the main hangers. I can't see much – I'm slowing to half speed.'

'Scout three, this is Delphine, Ana, have you ramped up to full beam? I know it'll cut your flight time but I don't want you taking any chances – we don't know what they left behind.'

'I'm on full beam, Ali, but this place is huge... Just a minute, something's coming in to view.'

'What is it?'

'It's nothing, just a mooring arm.' A further hour passed in relative silence as Ana surveyed her assigned section of Olympus Shipyard.

Once her survey was complete she returned to the launch bay of Delphine; the survey vessel to which she was assigned. Once she had docked she made her way to the briefing room.

Like everything on the corvette, the briefing room was small and compact. By the time she arrived, Ali, the ship's master, was already there along with the three other scouts.

'Sorry I'm late,' she said as she ordered a cup of tea from the small drinks machine in the corner of the room.

'I presume you ran your power cell pretty much flat again?' Ali asked.

'It was a large hanger; I didn't want to miss anything.'
'And did you?'
'Oh, no – they took *everything* with them when they left – it's just a shell now.'

'Did you guys find anything?' Ana asked the other scouts.

'No. Everything's been stripped bare,' a tall athletic man replied. He ran his fingers through his short dark hair. 'There's nothing we can use,' he sighed.

Ana traced the pattern of the vine tattoo that ran from the side of his face and down his neck with her eyes. '*I wonder how far down that goes.*'

'Dan's right; from what we've seen so far, and from what I've heard from the other surveys, the Settlers took everything they could with them when they left,' Ali said.

'Well at least we won't have to strip anything out if we want to recommission it,' another of Ali's scouts, a young dark-skinned woman, added.

'That's true enough, Sarah. I'd like to have *something* positive to report when we return to Luna,' Ali agreed. 'And speaking of which, here's the last area we're to survey.' Delphine's master called up an outline of a section of Olympus on the room's wall-mounted monitor.

'Is that all we've got?' a tall, heavy set man – the fourth of the ship's scouts – asked.

'Unfortunately, Ray, this section was built by the Settlers after the split, so we haven't got detailed plans. You'll just have to go carefully.'

Great, though I doubt we'll find anything more than we have so far,' Ray replied as he pushed back his chair and pulled himself out of it. '*Damned crappy standard size furniture.*'

'You're probably right, but we've got our orders,' Ali replied.

'I know; I'm not complaining, it's just that the Settler rebellion set us back so far,' Ray replied as he ordered a large carbonated fruit juice from the drinks machine.

'Which is why our job is so important. If we can recommission Olympus we'll have the space to begin the migration,' Sarah said.

'We've got the transports, but we can't begin ferrying people up to the moon yet. Ten city-ships are ready but the other eight aren't finished yet, and besides the whole of Luna is one huge shipyard – it couldn't handle the migration.' Ali added. 'So, shall we go and see whether this derelict can be put to good use?'

'Sounds like a plan to me,' Ray replied as he drained his drink.

***

The approach lanes to the moon were always congested; they had been ever since the Settler fleet had departed. President Jacob's shuttle had been queued behind a bulk carrier for the past hour waiting for clearance to approach Luna and dock. Eventually the carrier was directed to a vacant dock and the president's shuttle was directed to an available berth in Luna's shuttle bay.

As soon as the shuttle's hatch had opened a smartly dressed woman backed out onto the shuttle bay's deck carrying one end of a long ramp. Once she had set it down a man followed her and waited as President Jacobs disembarked. The president's wheelchair rolled smoothly down the ramp followed by half a dozen suited men and women.

'Mr President, the masters of the survey vessels that were sent out to Olympus are assembled in conference room four, as you requested,' a blustering man announced as President Jacobs left the shuttle bay.

'Thank you, Wilkins. I'll see them immediately.'

'Sir, I can have them wait a while; you needn't see them right away.'

'I've just launched the Eclipse, Wilkins, not run a marathon. I will see them now – I'm sure they're just as busy as you or I and haven't got time to waste waiting around in a conference room for no good reason,' the president snapped. It wasn't that launching Eclipse – the latest city-ship to be completed – had been a taxing affair; it hadn't. It was the implication that his disability somehow prevented him from discharging his duties as president to the full that angered him. He had been bed-ridden for months after being shot by his prime minister. It had taken him even longer to come to terms with the fact that he was now paralysed from the waist down: Prime Minister Taylor's shot had almost severed his spinal cord. The doctors had said that he had been exceedingly lucky to have any motor or sensory function at all. For a man who had always been highly active, being told that he was lucky to still be able to defecate of his own accord was little consolation. Any reference to his disability was usually met with a harsh retort.

Luna's administrative wing was quite some distance from the shuttle bay and it took the presidential party some time to traverse the busy lunar base. At length they reached conference room 4.

'I'm sorry to have kept you waiting. I'll try to keep this as brief as possible – I'm sure you all have other places you'd rather be.' As the president aligned his chair with the edge of the table the gathered masters took their seats. 'Now, what's left of Olympus?'

'Very little to be honest, Mr President; the main hangers are little more than shells I'm afraid.'

The president glanced at a screen built into the arm of his chair for a second. 'What *exactly* did the Settlers leave, Mr Kazmi?'

'Nothing other than the mooring arms, I'm afraid, Mr President,' Ali replied.

'So we can dock ships in the hangers then?'

'Yes, but—'

'That is good. Now, who performed the atmospheric survey?'

'That would be me, Mr President – Mr—'

'Mr Moser of the Pioneer. Please, go ahead.'

'Most of the shipyard is still airtight, Mr President. Only a few sections are evacuated.'

'Do they appear easily repairable?'

'Yes, Sir.'

'Mr President, Mr Kazmi is right when he said that they left little more than a shell. I inventoried the storage bays. They're bare, Sir; there's nothing – no spare parts for the station, no weapons, no fuel, nothing. Look,' a short, portly man replied before passing a tablet along the table to the president who skimmed it.

'Whilst I appreciate the thoroughness of your report, Mr Roberts, I must remind you that we are constructing a civilian fleet, *not* a naval one.'

'But surely, Mr President, what about self defence?'

'With the United Industries and the Settlers gone, we have a singular opportunity, an opportunity for a completely new start. I ask you, all of you, is there one man or woman here who would describe themselves as inherently violent?'

Silence.

'What's left of the humanity is tired of endless violence – we don't need weapons anymore, Mr Roberts.'

'I'm sorry, Mr President, I guess I'm still a little paranoid, what with the Settler rebellion and all.'

'That's understandable. I think we're all a bit nervous about taking such a big step – violence has been humanity's companion for so long we've almost forgotten how to live without it. But I believe it's possible, I really do.' Turning to address everyone President Jacobs continued. 'I'm aware that you have all submitted extensive reports on your surveys, but I'd like to know, do *you* think it's possible to convert Olympus into an embarkation port?' One by one everyone gave their assent. 'Thank you all, thank you. That will be all. You are excused.'

As the conference room emptied, President Jacobs motioned for one of his aides to approach. 'I want to see the minister for construction in my office as soon as possible, Kate; this is the end of the beginning.'

***

They were right; it was possible to convert what remained of Olympus Shipyard into an embarkation port. It was eighteen months before the port was operational, and even then there wasn't a single luxury to be found on the whole station. By this time all but one of the city-ships had been completed and work was well under way constructing the vast support fleet that would be required to supply and maintain them. Colossal agri-ships were constructed as well as gargantuan mining dreadnoughts, tankers, cargo freighters, sleek scout cutters and a myriad of other vessels.

As soon as Olympus was operational the final evacuation of Earth began. Every atmosphere-capable ship was involved, either in ferrying the remnant of Earth's population to Olympus, or in scouring the planet for isolated settlements. One by one the city-ships were populated until everyone who could be found and convinced to leave had done so. What remained of the planet's devastated flora and fauna was transported aboard the agri-ships once they were completed. The last task was to load the cargo freighters and fuel tankers. It took several months to fill the freighters' holds. During this time thousands of ship-loads of sea water were transported to the tankers.

At length, many years after the fifth post-exodus global summit had catalysed the second exodus, President Jacobs sat on the bridge of Dauntless, the last of the city-ships to be completed, and watched as a freighter transported the last shipment of water to the tankers.

'What have we done?' he asked no one in particular.

'Sir?' an aide asked.

'Have you ever seen any of the ancient pictures of Earth, the first ones to be taken from orbit?

'No, Sir, I haven't'

'They were beautiful; vibrant blues and greens covered in snow white clouds. Look at it now... we killed her, Wilkins; we killed our planet. I just pray we've learned our lesson.'

'I didn't know you were religious, Sir.'

'I'm not – it's a turn of phrase.' The president turned away from the viewing port and directed his wheelchair between the bustling bridge crew until he reached the captain's station. 'Get us out of here, Captain, I can't bear to look at her anymore.'

'Would you like to address the fleet, Mr President? This is a momentous occasion.'

'What would I say?'

'I don't know, Sir.'

'Exactly. Just get us out of here,' he replied, as his eyes welled up.

'Very well, Sir.'

And so, with little ceremony, the remnants of humanity, aboard eighteen city-ships and numerous smaller support vessels, departed their ravaged home-world for good.

***

It took several months for life on board the city-ships to settle down into something resembling normality. This was partly due to the gradual realisation by those that comprised the remnants of humanity that they were now nomads with nowhere to call home. By the time the fleet crossed the heliopause, entered inter-stellar space and left all traces of humanity's shameful, violence-ridden past behind, a sense of hope was beginning to emerge throughout the fleet.

The initial journey across the solar system was undertaken slowly; President Jacobs and his government felt that it was important for everyone to adjust to their new way of life before subjecting them to the unknown challenges of life in inter-stellar space. Once the heliopause had been crossed, the fleet gradually increased speed until it was travelling at full speed towards the nearest star system: Alpha Centauri. The fleet's city-ships could travel at eight-tenths the speed of light, much faster than most of their support vessels. Those vessels that could not cruise at 0.8c were forced to dock with their parent ship before it started its acceleration. When it came to maintaining the fleet there was no shortage of volunteers – everyone wanted to be a part of humanity's future.

Three years and four months after entering inter-stellar space, the fleet approached its first port of call; Proxima Centauri. Initially it was hoped that the fleet could enter orbit around this small star whilst surveys and studies were made of the rest of the Alpha Centauri system. Unfortunately the star's tendency to randomly and violently flare meant that this was not possible. In the end the fleet put into orbit around the Alpha Centauri AB binary system instead. Once in orbit, each city-ship dispatched their survey vessels to search for suitable sources of raw materials.

***

Along with Eclipse's eleven other survey vessels, Delphine had put to space shortly after the fleet had entered orbit and headed towards her designated coordinates. Ali Kazmi, the ship's master, had initially been very excited about surveying a hitherto unknown planet. Several weeks out from Eclipse, however, his fervour for exploration began to wane; he had grown accustomed to life aboard the city-ship with its bustling crowds and constant activity.

'It's lonely out here,' he reflected as Delphine finally reached her destination; αCenA1, a small rocky planet orbiting Alpha Centauri A. The delicate patter of finger tips on a console was the only thing that broke the silence on the bridge.

'What have we got, Ray?' Ali asked, setting his coffee cup down.

'Not a lot, to be honest – the atmosphere's messing with our scanners.'

'You can't get anything at all?'

'Not beyond the make up of those storm clouds. They're predominantly carbon dioxide, sulphuric acid and a number of other carbonates and silicates.'

'I would have thought our scanners could penetrate that.'

'Ordinarily they'd be able to, the readings would be a bit fuzzy, but they'd be able to. It's the storms we can't see through; there's too much electrical activity.'

'How much of the surface is affected?'

'About eighty per cent.'

'Damn. We're going to have to take her down. Gwyn, prepare for atmospheric flight.'

'Yes, Sir,' Ali's first mate replied.

Several minutes later Delphine entered the muddy-brown atmosphere of αCenA1. As she descended she was wracked by lightning strikes and winds of more than a hundred miles per hour. Eventually she dropped below the storm clouds and into the only slightly less inhospitable lower troposphere. The landscape was a barren, blasted wasteland of rocks and dust, all pale yellow.

'I'm still reading winds of eighty miles per hour out there, Sir, gusting to a hundred and twenty,' Ray reported, anxiety clear in his voice.

'It's okay, Ray, I'm not going to send you out in that; we'll complete the survey from here.'

'I'm not sure how long we can realistically remain in this atmosphere, Sir; undertaking the entire survey from here will take twice as long as if we send the scouts out,' Gwyn put in.

'I'm aware of that, but I'm not going to put Ray, or any of the others at risk by sending them out in that storm. We'll do what we can from here; send out the drones to collect samples.'

'Aye aye, Sir,' Gwyn replied.

Ray released the breath he hadn't been aware he had been holding and relaxed, as much as he could, into his chair. A few seconds later Delphine's four scout drones were launched into the storm. On the bridge Ray, Dan, Sarah and Ana fought to keep their respective drones airborne.

'How's it going?' Ali asked after several tense minutes.

'We're still airborne, barely.'

'What about samples?'

'Atmospheric samples aren't going to be a problem, but surface ones might be,' Ana replied.

'Do you think you'll be able to reach the surface?'

'No problem – whether you'll have any drones left afterwards is another matter though…' Sarah's voice trailed off as she fought to keep her drone airborne.

'Alright, for now just concentrate on acquiring surface scans. It might be that we'll find somewhere sheltered enough to set down and take some samples.' Four distracted grunts were the only reply Delphine's master got.

Half an hour passed in silence as the four scout drones gathered detailed telemetry of the planet's surface.

'That's odd…' Ray muttered.

'What?' Ali asked.

'The shape of these valleys…'

'What about them?'

'They're straight.'

'So what?' Dan asked without taking his eyes from his console.

'I mean they're dead straight; take a look.'

Beyond Earth: New Earth

Dan tapped an icon in the corner of his screen and called up the view from Ray's drone. 'That *is* odd, it's almost like—' the scout was cut off mid-sentence as a series of alarms sounded from his console. He swore as the view from his drone showed a chaos of swirling storm clouds. 'Damn it!'

'What happened?' Ali asked, crossing the bridge to the scout's terminal.

'It must have been a squall or something; the drone's gone into a spin. I think I can—' The view from the drone's camera suddenly showed a vast yellow-brown rock face and then went black. 'DAMN IT!' Dan kicked his terminal's mount in frustration and then immediately regretted it as pain shot through his foot.

'Dan, calm down. Okay, Ana, Sarah, bring your drones back to the ship. Ray...' Ali's gaze settled on the view being projected from Ray's drone.

'Do you want me back too?'

'No, I want as much information as possible on... whatever that is.'

'Dan limped over to Ray. 'That can't be natural; it's *too* straight.'

'It has to be,' Ray countered.

'Have you ever seen anything like it? Ever?' Dan asked.

'Well, no...'

'Well if it's not a natural phenomenon, what? ' Ali began.

'Don't you mean who? ' Dan replied.

'Just a moment, I'm close enough now to switch to the high-resolution camera.'

'Those grooves,' Dan gasped, 'they've got to be—'

'But the Settlers were heading to New Earth; they can't have ended up here, surely...' Ali interrupted.

'That's not where I was going.'

'Don't say it, Dan, don't say it,' Ali whispered.

'Do you want me to try and set down and get some surface samples?'

'No, return to the ship; I want to be back on Eclipse as soon as possible.'

Once the three remaining scout drones had been recovered the journey back to Eclipse, all three weeks of it, was haunted by a spectre of foreboding. Upon their return, this sense of apprehension escalated to one of outright dread as they heard similar reports from other returning survey vessels. Before long sinister rumours began spreading through the fleet. At length President Jacobs and his government were able to restore some semblance of calm to the terrified populace. The signs of alien life, they were assured, were extremely old; there was no evidence of recent activity. A return to the bright, optimistic days prior to reaching Alpha Centauri might have been possible if it weren't for the gagging order placed on the crews of the fleet's survey vessels. They were forbidden from talking about what they had seen in order to prevent fallacious rumours spreading disquiet and paranoia amongst the fleet. And so a pall of nervous anxiety settled over the Nomad fleet.

It was initially intended that the fleet remain in orbit around Alpha Centauri for quite some time in order to make a full survey of Earth's nearest planetary system. It soon became clear, however, that if another outbreak of near-crippling anxiety was to be avoided, the fleet should re-supply and leave the system as soon as possible.

As preparations were being made to break orbit President Jacobs addressed the fleet. 'For so long we were masters of all we surveyed; little was unknown to us. Now, however, as we venture out of our solar system for the first time, we are discovering that, whilst our knowledge is great, there is infinitely more to learn. We have always known this, of course, but we are now experiencing the reality of it for the first time. It might be a shock at first, but it need not be something to fear; rather something to be embraced with a child-like curiosity – how much more there is to learn! Friends, you need not fear the unknown;

you are not venturing into it alone. Together we stare it full in the face and do not shrink back, but rather ask, 'what are you hiding?'. At 22:30 we depart Alpha Centauri for a star system that doesn't even have a name. What a time to be alive!'

Once the fleet had departed Alpha Centauri and returned to inter-stellar space the atmosphere improved. People began to embrace the notion that they were now a race of explorers, each with their own role to play in peeling back the layers of the unknown to peer beneath. There were, of course, a few exceptions. Master Ali was one such soul. He was not convinced that what they had seen on αCenA1 was as old as they had been assured. He would stay up into the early hours poring over the telemetry that Ray's drone had recorded. The idea that what they had seen were little more than the last vestiges of a long-extinct civilisation didn't sit well with him. His fears and anxieties were unpopular, however, so he kept them to himself.

***

At 09:30 fleet-time President Jacobs entered Eclipse's bridge as he had done every morning for five and a half years: ever since the fleet had entered inter-stellar space. He was, as usual, warmly received.

'Good morning, Harry. Congratulations again. How are you this morning?' Captain Lewis asked as the president, concluding his tour of the bridge, wheeled up to the command deck.

'James, good morning. Thank you. Me? You know me – I gave up partying into the small hours years ago! Seriously though, I never expected to live to see this,' he replied, gesturing to the main screen that was projecting a view of Eclipse's bow and the void beyond. 'Never mind being re-elected three times!'

'The people have spoken, Harry: they know that you'll—-'

'Captain, I'm getting a strange reading on the long-range scanners, approaching from the port bow,' one of the bridge crew interrupted.

'What is it, Hendricks?' the captain replied.

'I'm not sure, Sir. It looks like…'

'Go on, don't be shy just because the president's here.'

'Well, Sir, it looks an awful lot like…'

'Mr Hendricks?'

'Well, Mr President, it looks an awful lot like another ship, Sir.'

'That can't be right. You must have misinterpreted the signal,' the captain replied, striding over to Hendricks' station. 'That does look… Run another scan,' he said, his eyes glued to the console. President Jacobs wheeled over whilst the long-range scanners re-scanned the closing contact.

'It's the same, Sir.' The alarm in Hendricks' voice was almost palpable.

The captain turned to the president. 'Harry, what should I do?'

President Harry Jacobs was silent for several minutes before he finally replied in hushed tones. 'Signal the fleet, bring us into close order.'

'That's it?'

'What else can we do? Pray? We left God back on Earth, James – it's just us now.' There was a disquiet in the president's tone that spoke of a long held belief suddenly shattered.

'What if they're hostile?' a nearby bridge-crewman asked no one in particular.

'Then we're all dead: we've got a few mass drivers scattered across the dreadnoughts, but nothing else,' another replied.

'That may be our one saving grace, Mrs King. We have a sad history of violence in first contact situations. The results were invariably tragic. Perhaps now we have a chance to prove that we really have moved on as a race,' the president replied, his voice low.

'But what if they are hostile?' Captain Lewis asked.

'Game over.' Hendricks whispered.

The next half an hour passed in tense silence as the unidentified vessel approached the fleet, heading straight for Eclipse.

'The short-range scanners are now in range, Captain,' one of the bridge crew reported.

'Put it on the main screen.' Lewis replied curtly.

Slowly the vessel came into focus. With a gently curved bow, it was twice as long as it was wide with a uniform cross-section along its length. As it approached it began to decelerate.

'Julian, order the fleet to match our speed,' the captain ordered.

'Aye aye, Sir,' Commander Julian Waters, his second-in-command replied.

'Helmsman, reduce our speed to match that of the approaching vessel,' Lewis continued.

'Aye aye, Sir,' the helmsman replied.

Slowly and cautiously the Nomad fleet slowed until its lead ship, Eclipse, was no more than a few thousand kilometres from the, now stationary, alien ship. From this distance the bulbous protrusions that covered the vessel's hull were clearly visible, as was its colour: a pale metallic blue.

'Sir, we're getting a broad spectrum incoming transmission,' a bridge hand reported with a voice that was threatening to break with nerves.

'How?'

'Let's hear it,' President Jacobs said as Eclipse's captain mouthed unanswerable questions.

A few seconds later the transmission, in broken English, was relayed across the bridge speakers. 'Inhabitants from Earth,' an unnerving, damp voice began, 'we, of the Yr N'gith League, through me, Chu'l G'nith, welcome you with a hand outstretched, which is peace. If you would like to communicate with visual as well as audible senses, please reply appropriately: we have the technology.' Eclipse's bridge was silent for a long time.

'James, prepare for a visual transmission,' President Jacobs said at length.

'Harry, are you sure? I mean—'

'That wasn't a question, Captain. This is my responsibility; it's what I was elected for.'

'Okay, erm... Right, You'll need to be on the command deck,' the captain stammered.

'That's *yes, Mr President,* Captain. Try and remain calm, Captain; your crew are depending on you as the fleet is depending on me.'

'I'm sorry, Sir, it's just... How can you be sure their intentions really are peaceful?'

'I can't; now please, the transmission, Captain,' the president replied as he wheeled to the command deck.

'Yes, Mr President. It's ready when you are.'

'Then begin transmission, Captain.' President Jacobs paused, sat up in his wheelchair and then began his address. 'Chuool Genith of the Ear In-Gith League,' he began, struggling with the alien pronunciation, 'I, President Harry Jacobs, bring you greetings from the human race, formerly of Earth.' President Jacobs paused. '*Keep it short and sweet.'* After a couple of seconds he made up his mind, motioned to Captain Lewis to cease transmitting, sunk back into his chair and sighed deeply.

A few minutes later Eclipse's bridge received a response. Captain Lewis, after an uncharacteristic show of uncertainty, ordered for it to be accepted and relayed via one of the bridge's screens. The creature that filled the screen was beyond anything anyone on the bridge had ever imagined, even in their worst fever dreams. What passed for the creature's head was bulbous and featureless with the exception of two long and four shorter protrusions that were reminiscent of mandibles, though the creature had no obvious mouth. Little was visible of the creature below its head, but what could be seen stilled the hearts of Eclipse's bridge crew. Most of the it was covered in what appeared to be turquoise scales. Beneath the scales a biomechanical construct was visible, underneath which a dark purple-black mass was evident.

'President Jacobs, it is our honour to meet you. We have been long hoping for this moment,' the creature replied.

'You have been waiting for us to leave Earth for a long time? How long have you known of our existence?'

'Members of the Yr N'gith League have been aware of your race for about one hundred and ninety thousand Earth cycles.'

'But you've never made contact before?'

'No.'

'Why?'

'You were not ready. You could not live in harmony. You're focus was too close.'

President Jacobs paused for a moment before laughing.

'Is this funny to you, President Jacobs?'

'I'm sorry, no. Our past is no joke. It is simply a bitter truth that we have had to suffer so much to learn so simple a lesson.'

'Yet, still you laugh. Why?'

'We call it humour: it is a complex concept to explain.'

'It would be useful to meet head-to-head, as you say.'

'Face-to-face. Yes, I think that would be useful. Where would you suggest,' the president stammered, his mouth bone dry.

'You are fearful, President Jacobs? That is expected. We have met many races for the first time. We can send one over to you. Alone. Would that calm you?'

'Er, yes. Please, I will need time to organise a dock…There are preparations that need to be made.'

'Of course. You have the time, President Jacobs. We will wait. You will prepare, then you will inform us, and then we will come to you.'

There was silence across the bridge for some minutes before the president broke it. 'Vice-president Andrews, may I assume you are aware of our situation?' he said, speaking into a microphone mounted on his wheelchair.

'President Jacobs; the initial message was transmitted across a broad spectrum with no encryption, but I've heard nothing more.' The vice-president's usually clipped, confident tone betrayed more than a hint of consternation.

'We are meeting them, Vice-president, on our terms, on a vessel of our choice, when we're ready. Please organise a special session to convene at once.'

'We're *what*? Mr President, you don't have the authority! How do we know that their intentions are peaceful? You—'

'Vice-president Andrews, I *do* have the authority. I may not have exercised it before, but I am now. Have faith, Marta. Please do as I ask; I don't like giving orders.'

'… Very well, Mr President. I will organise for the session to convene in one hour.'

'Thank you.' The president cut the link and looked up at Captain Lewis.

'I hope you know what you're doing, Harry,' the captain said in hushed tones.

'So do I, my friend, so do I.'

The special session was, as it turned out, little more than a formality thanks to the president's rash acceptance of the alien's suggestion of a face-to-face meeting. In fact the first half of the session consisted of little more than the assembled councillors expressing their displeasure at the president's recent actions. Eventually, however, once everyone had had an opportunity to express themselves the matter at hand was discussed. After a short debate, it was agreed that the initial meeting should take place at noon the following day in the largest of Eclipse's docking bays.

Beyond Earth: New Earth

The following day, at the appointed hour, the alien emissary arrived at Eclipse's third starboard dock, which had previously been cleared of all docked vessels. The emissary's vessel was similar in colour and design to the parent ship; pale metallic blue, long, oval in cross-section and covered in bulbous protrusions. It differed from its parent vessel in one detail: a long, multi-jointed arm extended from the ship's starboard bow. This extension proved to be the vessel's mooring arm; as the small ship approached the designated bay, the arm extended, rotated and acquired a seal with the bay's docking ring.

The tension in dock three was so thick it was almost tangible as bay five's iris door opened. To President Jacobs the creature that entered the dock was the same one he had been conversing with the previous day. Now, however, he wasn't just conversing with a view screen and the reality of the situation hit him hard. His heart began thumping in his chest and his mouth dried as the emissary skittered towards him. At eight feet tall Chu'l G'nith towered above the tallest of the gathered delegation. The creature's biomechanical skeleton extended below the mass of scale-covered purple-black tissue which made up its main bulk to form a set of eight highly dexterous legs. The ten multi-jointed limbs that protruded in all directions from the creature's main bulk ended in what appeared to be sucker cups or toothless maws and appeared to taste the air as it crossed the docking bay towards President Jacobs.

'President Jacobs, I experience pleasure at meeting you now. For the first time.' Chu'l G'nith's voice was no less damp or unnerving now than it had been in the earlier transmissions.

'Chuool Genith, it is likewise a pleasure to meet you in... person,' the president stammered.

'Please, President, feel free to utilise your syntax. It is my experience that it helps greatly in situations such as this.'

'Er, well, thank you. Is everything alright for you? The atmosphere I mean. I hadn't expected you to breathe oxygen.'

'Breathe? Ah, yes: to respire. I do not respire as you understand the concept. I absorb what I need through my Noitalmu.' Chu'l G'nith gestured with one of its limbs to its scales. 'We are... symbiotes, I think you would say. We are spawned with a small number but over our lifespans they multiply until they cover our entire outer membrane. To answer your question, everything I need to survive in your atmosphere is supplied by nutrient tanks attached to my lower exoskeleton.' From his position President Jacobs could see two semi-spherical devices attached the the underside of Chu'l G'nith's exoskeleton where the legs joined the main structure.

'I hope you will forgive me: normally I would offer you refreshment, but I have no idea what to offer...' the president said, trying to draw as little attention as possible to the fact that he felt deeply uncomfortable with Chu'l G'nith's lack of face.

'There is nothing to forgive because you could have done nothing more than you have. It is an honour that so many of you are present at this meeting.'

'Is that not usually the case?'

'No. It is what happens normally that only one or two will meet with me at first.'

'Well, it is our custom to present the most important members of our society to visiting dignitaries. In this case it is my pleasure to present my entire cabinet as well as our leading scientists. Please, allow me to introduce you to them.' The president began to relax slightly as proceedings entered better known territory.

It took more than an hour for the president to introduce everyone to Chu'l G'nith: the emissary would often stop to question a councillor about their role or some other, apparently trivial, matter. Eventually, however, the introductions were complete and proceedings once again entered uncharted territory.

President Jacobs paused after the last dignitary had been introduced, unsure what to say.

'May I make a suggestion, President?' Chu'l G'nith asked.

'Of, of course,' the president stammered.

'You will all have many questions, I am sure,' Chu'l G'nith began, addressing the entire assembly. 'I propose a second meeting. You are all, as many as are willing, welcome to my vessel to meet representatives of my ship's crew.' Immediately the offer was made shocked whispering spread across the dock. 'You have nothing to fear. I will gladly stay here as a... I am sorry, I do not know the correct term.'

'Hostage,' a councillor offered.

'As a hostage then: I will remain aboard while you are aboard my vessel as a gesture of good faith.'

The whispering subsided and the president turned to address those gathered in the dock. 'I will not be drawn into a lengthy debate. All those in favour of Chool Genith's proposal raise your hands.' At first only one or two hands were raised, and those cautiously. At length every hand was raised: curiosity had gotten the better of fear.

'I will return to my ship until you are ready to come over: I only have a limited supply of nutrients.'

'Very well, Chool Genith. We will contact you when we are ready to come over,' the president said, smiling for the first time in two days. 'I believe this has been a great success,' he continued, offering his hand. An embarrassing silence followed. 'I'm sorry, it is customary for us to shake hands as a sign of good faith and friendship...' the president trailed off, unsure how to continue without seeming rude.

'Do not be embarrassed, President Jacobs. Will this satisfy your customs to a satisfactory degree?' Chu'l G'nith extended one of its limbs and placed the sucker in the palm of the president's outstretched hand. The president could not cover an involuntary wince as the alien's cup latched on to his hand. Chu'l G'nith appeared not to notice, however.

'I hope this will be the first of many signs of good faith and friendship, President Jacobs,' the emissary said as it withdrew its limb and returned to its ship. Once the iris door had sealed the docking bay erupted into a cacophony of conversation.

***

Order wasn't restored to the third starboard dock for another hour. Eventually, however, President Jacobs found himself presiding over another, this time impromptu, special session. Unlike the previous day's session this one was far more positive; meeting with Chu'l G'nith had had a significant impact on those present. President Jacobs informed the alien emissary that those currently present had all accepted its invitation visit its ship. The president was in turn informed that the visit could commence presently: their acceptance of the invitation had been anticipated.

A flight of shuttles were brought round to the dock three, the assembly boarded, and they proceeded to follow Chu'l G'nith's ship back to its waiting parent vessel. The emissary's ship led the following shuttles into a long bay which was open to space at both ends. As the last of the shuttles entered the bay the alien's ship returned to space and returned to Eclipse as a hostage, as had been agreed.

Once all the vessels had landed in the alien docking bay doors slid down across both ends of the bay, sealing it from space.

'I'm reading a change in the atmosphere outside, Mr President,' the pilot of the president's shuttle announced a few seconds after the bay doors closed. 'Twenty-one per cent oxygen, seventy-eight per cent nitrogen… I don't believe it, Mr President; the composition is almost exactly the same as—'

'Earth. That doesn't surprise me; they appear to know a great deal about us. Continue monitoring the atmosphere and let me know when it is safe to disembark.'

'Yes, Sir.'

A couple of minutes later the pilot announced that the pressure outside had reached 1 atmosphere and was remaining constant. No one disembarked from any of the shuttles for several minutes. Eventually President Jacobs took the initiative and ordered his shuttle to disembark.

Chu'l G'nith was waiting for him as he wheeled down the disembarkation ramp. 'I am glad you accepted my invitation, President Jacobs. The others will be here shortly.'

Cautiously the rest of the company disembarked from their respective shuttles and began looking around with open mouths, incredulous at what they were seeing. There was little to distinguish the walls, ceiling and the deck from each other: they were all the same pale metallic blue as the outside of the ship and all appeared somewhat organic in nature, though as hard and cold as steel to the touch.

About ten minutes after the company from Eclipse had disembarked an opening appeared in the side of the bay. Part door, part orifice, it expanded until it was wide enough to permit a number of aliens, all clearly the same species as Chu'l G'nith, to pass through into the bay. Around fifty aliens processed into the bay and began mingling with President Jacobs and his company.

Over the next couple of hours any latent reservations the human party may have had were laid to rest. The Yr N'gith League, it was discovered, was a union of two-dozen alien races who had come together for mutual support and co-operation. Chu'l G'nith's race, the Heí, came from a very low gravity world and so had developed space-faring vessels with very low artificial gravity. This meant that once they had been accepted into the league, they could not easily interact with its other members who were all from higher gravity home-worlds. A team of the league's leading scientists therefore developed exoskeletons for them that allowed them to exist in much higher gravity environments.

It gradually became clear that the League had a strict policy of not interacting with alien races until they had reached a certain degree of advancement. This advancement, it was discovered, was not measured simply in technological terms: if it was, the League would have sent a delegation to Earth many years ago. According to Chu'l G'nith, it was only recently, having cast off the last vestiges of its selfish, greed-tainted, violent past that humanity had advanced far enough to be invited to join the League.

'How would we go about joining the League?' President Jacobs asked one of Chu'l G'nith's companions, one Ghu'n G'nar.

'It is an extensive process, though not overly lengthy,' the alien replied.

'Can that process begin here?'

'Your eagerness to join us is commendable, President; however, the application progress must be conducted on a home-world. The nearest is our own, approximately two-hundred and thirty light years from here.'

The president's heart sunk. At full speed the fleet could not reach the Heí home-world in much less than 290 years.

'Please, President Jacobs, do not fear. We are aware of your fleet's technological limitations. The rest of our fleet is waiting in the next star system; we have the capability to bring you all to Heí in a fraction of the time it would take you normally.'

'I don't understand.'

'Our larger ships have two drives: a sub-light drive that is similar in its capabilities to your own, and a hyper-gravity drive that enables us to reach speeds far in excess of the speed of light.' Recognising the look on the president's face, Ghu'n G'nar continued. 'It works by folding space-time, thus allowing our largest ships to travel vast distances in a fraction of the time that our smaller ships, with their conventional drives, are capable of.'

'And you could fit these drives to our city-ships?'

'No, President Jacobs, we could not: you are not yet a member of the League. What we can do is expand the hyper-gravity bubble each of our ships produce to encompass one or more of your vessels. In this way we would be able to transport your fleet to Heí in order for your application to the League to be processed. Incidentally, do you speak for the entire fleet?'

'I am its spokesperson and have certain powers, but all major decisions are made by the government, which is in turn democratically elected. If it were up to me, I would have you transport us to Heí immediately: I see this as the opportunity humanity has been waiting for; however, it is not up to me. I am afraid there will be no firm decisions made today, despite your warm welcome. The people must have an opportunity to consult with their councillors and then there must be a vote. It will not be a short process I'm afraid.'

'Do not be afraid, President Jacobs, decisions of such magnitude must not be rushed and your people must be consulted. I would expect nothing less from anyone who wished to join the League. We will provide you with the coordinates of the star system in which our fleet is currently waiting. Once you have made a decision you may join us there and we will either begin preparations for your transport to Heí, or we will part as friends and wish your race fortune and prosperity for the future.'

'Are you then empowered to speak for your government?'

'In a manner of speaking: we are a telepathic race and share a single, collective consciousness. We each speak on behalf of, and for, each other,' Ghu'n G'nar explained, looking round. Conversations were coming to an end and the aliens were beginning to leave the bay. 'I am afraid our nutrient tanks are beginning to run low. I have enjoyed our meeting, Mr President; I hope it will not be our last.'

'Nor I, Choon Genar,' the president replied, offering the palm of his hand. The alien touched it with the sucker of one of his limbs before turning and leaving the bay with the last of his companions. Once their hosts had departed the president and his party boarded their shuttles and waited for the atmosphere to be pumped out and the bay doors opened.

It would be a long and complex process to organise the referendum on whether or not humanity should join the Yr N'gith League, yet President Jacobs began planning it immediately. His enthusiasm was infectious and in less than a month consultations were being offered throughout the fleet: everyone was being given an opportunity to ask whatever questions they had. Even so, it was a full year before a formal vote could be organised. In truth it could have been undertaken earlier, but the president, and indeed most of his councillors, wanted as long as possible to talk those people round who still had reservations. And so it was that approximately a year after humanity's first contact with an alien species, a referendum was undertaken on whether it should apply for membership to the Yr N'gith League.

***

'It is with great joy that I can now announce the result of the referendum,' President Jacobs began from Eclipse's bridge. 'Votes for applying to join the Yr N'gith League, ninety-six per cent. Votes against joining the League, one per cent. Abstentions, three per cent.' The roar of celebration that erupted across the bridge was deafening. 'We will...' the president trailed off, drowned out by the cheering. 'We will,' he began again once the cheers had subsided, 'therefore, begin making preparations for immediate departure. Our destination will be the Heí fleet in the next star system, one point two light years away. There is much to be done in the next year and a half, but I'm sure that if we all work together we will arrive in the best possible shape to enter what I firmly believe to be the next great age of humanity!' Another great cheer erupted across the bridge, a cheer that was echoed across the bridge of every ship in the fleet.

Slowly, ponderously, the eighteen city-ships that contained the remnants of humanity cycled their drives to full power and made for the Heí fleet and a brighter future than any aboard had ever dared to hope for.

Dr S. Fern

TEMPORAL INVARIANCE

Some four month's journey from Nostrovka – the gateway station that stabilised the Russian Federation wormhole linking New Earth with The Field – the mining dreadnought Mariya Vasyev drifted slowly through the outer reaches of the Phoenix Nebula harvesting its mineral-rich gas and dust. Several hundred kilometres out from the dreadnought's port quarter the Corvette Askold kept pace, a silent escort in the vastness of the void.

'Lieutenant Solyakov, anything to report?' Captain-lieutenant Krastimir Strasky asked his chief navigation officer, the tone of his voice reflecting the tedium on the bridge.

'Nothing, sir – not that our sensors can detect much in this nebula,' the young woman replied, her tone betraying the deep-seated boredom that escort duties such as these always elicited.

The captain-lieutenant didn't bother responding. In The Field, escorting mining operations was imperative; 'accidents' were common place. Despite the abundance of resources, every alliance, union, and coalition were out for themselves – even the Kingdom of India had started throwing its weight around in recent years. So far out into the void however, all sense of the perpetual hostilities died away as monotonous week followed monotonous week. With little that required his attention, Captain-lieutenant Strasky found himself staring vacantly out into the vibrantly coloured nebula, waiting for his shift to end.

The lethargy that had settled across the bridge was suddenly banished as the Mariya Vasyev exploded, for a few seconds lighting up the darkness of space as her ion drives went critical.

'ALL STOP! SOUND THE ALARM!' Strasky bellowed, leaping from his chair. 'Lieutenant Solyakov, full sensor sweep; report contacts!' A tense minute passed as the vessel's sensors swept the void.

'Nothing, Sir – there's nothing out there.'

'Nonsense! A ship doesn't explode for no reason. Something *caused* it to blow up – I want to know what!'

Lieutenant Solyakov hesitated for a moment before replying, a look of confusion crossing her face, 'I'm not reading anything now but…'

'What is it, Lieutenant?'

'Well, Sir, it doesn't make much sense. At the exact moment of the explosion the sensors detected two objects, one moving towards us and the other away from us.'

'What were they?'

'I don't know, Sir, their respective blue and red-shifts are like nothing I've ever seen before.'

'A sensor malfunction perhaps?'

'No, Sir, absolutely not. The sensors are fine – I calibrated them myself at the beginning of my shift.' Captain-lieutenant Strasky grunted in acceptance – maintenance and equipment calibrations had been about all there had been to do for months now. 'This is strange, Sir,' the lieutenant continued as she manipulated the controls on her console, 'If I plot the course of the two objects based on their doppler shifts I get two linear trajectories, one that originated somewhere off our port quarter and another that impacted the Mariya Vasyev amidships.'

'Perhaps it was some aspect of the nebula we haven't encountered before? An explosive gas pocket perhaps?' one of the lieutenant's assistant navigators suggested.

'No, Osip, it doesn't read like an explosion, and besides these doppler shifts are far too large.'

Several minutes passed in silence as the crew of the Askold scoured the void as best they could, given the interference caused by the nebula.

'Vessel approaching off our port quarter, Sir!' Lieutenant Solyakov reported.

'Identification?' the captain-lieutenant enquired, suddenly tense.

'U.I. cruiser, call sign Tau-zero-five, configuration unknown.'

'Engage silent running. I knew it...' he spat as all of the corvette's systems except life-support and its manoeuvring thrusters were cycled down to minimum power.

***

'Vice-admiral Kurchov, I appreciate your making the time to join us – Nostrovka is a busy station. Your report was extremely thorough; you have my thanks,' Admiral Viktor Rudnikov said. The elderly admiral sat in a comfortable high-backed, leather chair. His office, situated within the Russian Federation Admiralty building on New Earth, was more crowded than usual with vice-admirals, counter-admirals as well as a couple of others who were clearly not naval officers. 'Ladies and gentlemen, I have convened this meeting because, as you can see from vice-admiral Kurchov's report, we have finally been fortunate enough to observe the cause of the losses we have been experiencing.'

'I thought it crucial to report as much detail as possible, given the number of *accidents* we have suffered in the last year,' Vice-admiral Kurchov began, turning to address the assembled flag officers. Her holographic image flickered.

'Three dreadnoughts, two heavy cruisers, two survey vessels and one processing station, in *eight months*, Vice-admiral,' a heavily bearded man, who also bore the markings of a vice-admiral, interjected.

'Eight months, my apologies, Vice-admiral Pogrovich.'

'Is this *all* Captain-lieutenant Strasky has to report?' one of the assembled counter-admirals asked, waving a tablet he was holding at the vice-admiral's hologram.

'I am afraid so, Sir. I haven't been able to debrief him yet – the Askold is still three and a half months away; however, I have no reason to doubt that the captain-lieutenant reported all that he could. As you have read, he was forced to engage silent running until the enemy vessel departed the area – he could not perform any sensor sweeps without risking revealing his position,' she replied.

'But what he reports makes no sense. Take the chronology of his report for example; if this U.I. crusier – the Tau-zero-five – was responsible for the destruction of the Mariya Vasyev, given that it arrived almost fifteen minutes *after* the dreadnought exploded, the range from which it opened fire would have to have been—'

'Accurately targeting from such a range is simply not possible,' another of the admiral's subordinates interrupted.

'And what about this report of simultaneous objects appearing at the time of the explosion. This has to be a sensor malfunction – nothing else makes sense,' Vice-admiral Pogrovich added.

'Object, singular, and it can make sense. If I may, Admiral?' a woman, one of the civilians, interrupted.

'Doctor Iknakov, certainly,' Admiral Rudnikov replied.

'The captain-lieutenant's reported sensor readings are a match with some research that was being carried out in my high energy laboratory a couple of years ago. I said object, *singular*, because that is what I believe the crew of the Askold witnessed – a single object originating from off their port-quarter, passing them, and subsequently impacting the Mariya Vasyev. Only an object travelling at a superluminal velocity would produce a signature like the one the captain-lieutenant observed. Such an object, would not be observable until *after* it had passed the observer, at which point it would be observed moving *away*. Hence, unobservable,' the doctor made a sweeping gesture with her right hand from her left side to her face, 'observable, both approaching and moving away,' the doctor now moved her hand to the right, completing her illustration.

'Impossible! Nothing can move faster than light!' another of the assembled flag officers stated.

'Not true – tachyons do, and we have observed in the laboratory precisely what Captain-lieutenant Strasky reported.'

'But something that's observable only after it has passed you by? It doesn't make sense.'

'If the object is moving faster than the light it is emitting, it will arrive at the observer *before* that light.' Silence reigned in the admiral's office for a couple of minutes whilst the assembled officers tried to absorb what the doctor had just said.

'What you are suggesting, Doctor, is that United Industries has developed a weapon that fires tachyon munitions?' Vice-admiral Kurchov's hologram asked, finally breaking the silence.

'Probably an energy lance of some kind.'

'You mean like a laser, but made of tachyons?'

'Just a minute. Are you suggesting, Doctor, that United Industries has a weapon that can target us from the *future*? That is ludicrous!' Vice-admiral Pogrovich laughed.

It's not ludicrous, Vice-admiral – I have personally observed such a thing, albeit on a smaller scale, in the laboratory. How manoeuvrable is a vessel like a mining dreadnought or one of your cruisers?'

'Compared to what?'

'How much could it alter its heading or speed in, say, fifteen minutes?'

'They aren't the most manoeuvrable vessels in the navy, why?'

'So if I know the heading and velocity of one of your cruisers, I could reasonably easily calculate where it would have been fifteen minutes ago, especially if it had no reason to change course?'

'I suppose so.'

'So if I know where your vessel was fifteen minutes ago and I have a munition that can travel, effectively back in time, I can open fire before it detects me – which is, in my opinion, what we have been witnessing.' The colour drained from Admiral Rudnikov's face.

'You keep referring to shifts of fifteen minutes, Doctor. Why?' Vice-admiral Kurchov asked.

'I suspect its temporal range would be limited to such a degree. You see, just as a massive particle's energy increases as its velocity increases, a tachyon's decreases: the faster it travels, the less energy it has.'

'So there is a limit to how far into the past the weapon can target before its energy is too low to constitute any real threat?' the vice-admiral's hologram asked, her flickering image beginning to betray a hint of comprehension.

'Just so, Vice-admiral. I would suggest that the fifteen minutes reported between the destruction of the Mariya Vasyev and the appearance of the U.I. cruiser provide us with a reasonably reliable approximation of the weapon's range.'

'So what do you suggest we do, Doctor?' another of the admiral's subordinates asked.

'I would suggest, Counter-admiral Milnikov, that you find this vessel before it finds you. Also, I would suggest that discovering as much about this new weapon as possible to be a priority – as I have said I oversaw some work in this area a couple of years ago, but it did not progress much beyond the experimental stages.'

'And how exactly would you suggest we *discover as much about this weapon as possible*?' the counter-admiral asked.

'That, Sir, I would suggest, is a task for our intelligence service.'

Thank you for your insights, Doctor. Vice-admiral Kurchov I want all escorts and patrols doubled. Commandeer vessels from the system fleets if necessary –

we can't afford to suffer any more *accidents*,' the admiral stated.

'Aye aye, Sir – I will see to it at once,' she replied before the admiral leaned over and cut the feed from Nostrovka Station. 'That will be all – thank you for your time,' he said, dismissing the assembled officers and scientists. As the last of his flag officers departed Admiral Rudnikov poured himself a glass of vodka. Doctor Ivnakov's suggestion that the enemy not only possessed a weapon that could target them from the future but was evidently field-testing it had unsettled him deeply. After taking a large draught of the potent spirit the admiral activated his intercom. 'Get me Colonel-general Zukov.'

'At once, Sir,' his secretary replied from the next room.

'Doctor Ivkakov was right – we must find out as much as we can about this weapon as soon as possible,' he thought to himself as he waited for his long-time friend, and deputy-director of the intelligence service, to arrive.

***

The amphitheatre-like bridge of Nostrovka Gateway Station was enormous; hundreds of ratings overseen by dozens of non-commissioned officers ensured that the station was always operating at maximum efficiency. Vice-admiral Kurchov leaned on the railing that encompassed the command deck, enjoying a brief moment to herself.

'Vice-admiral, I have a priority message from the Aleksei Garin – a Kazan class cruiser currently acting as escort to a dreadnought in sector thirty-five.'

'Transfer it to one of the main screens.'

After a slight delay one of the large view screens that lined the rear wall of the command deck switched from projecting a view of the wormhole to one of the Aleksei Garin. The flickering image showed mostly smoke and the occasional flicker of flame.

A couple of seconds after later a badly burnt officer came into view. 'This is Lieutenant Ilnyev of the cruiser Aleksei Garin. All of the bridge officers are dead – I am commanding the ship from fire control. Ten minutes ago an explosion off our starboard bow destroyed the bridge, the forward turrets and voided most of the bow. I am attaching our exact coordinates and current status to this message. Please send help.'

The vice-admiral turned to another of her lieutenants. 'What was their last known location?'

'The edge of the Pegasus Nebula,' the lieutenant replied as she projected a view of the nebula onto another screen, 'the last known location of the Aleksei Garin is here.' A red dot appeared at the edge of the nebula.

'How far away is that?'

'It depends, a corvette could reach the nebula in about a week, a cruiser class vessel would take about nine days, a battleship—'

'Thank you, Lieutenant. Is Captain-lieutenant Strasky still aboard?'

The lieutenant tapped away at her console for a second, 'Yes, Vice-admiral. He is currently on recreation deck two.'

'Have him report to my office immediately.'

Ten minutes later Captain-lieutenant Strasky was admitted to the vice-admiral's office.

'You wished to see me, Vice-admiral?'

'Yes, than you for coming,' she replied, rising and returning the captain-lieutenant's salute.

'Is something wrong, Vice-admiral?' Strasky asked.

'One of our cruisers has been crippled on the outskirts of the Pegasus Nebula.'

'And you suspect the Tau-zero-five?'

'Yes, Captain-lieutenant, I do.'

'If I may speak freely?'

'Of course.'

Beyond Earth: New Earth

'My crew have only just returned and, to be honest, I'm not sure how you expect a corvette to hunt a vessel as formidable as the Tau-zero-five – if I have understood your reason for this meeting correctly?'

'You are very astute, Captain-lieutenant. Given that you are the only person to have survived an encounter with this vessel, I deem you to be the best equipped to hunt it down. Admiral Rudnikov has informed me that he is trying to learn as much about the Tau-zero-five as possible; however, such information takes time to acquire and time is something we do not have.'

'But, Vice-admiral, I only command a corvette – I appreciate the honour you are bestowing on me, but you must realise—'

'I do, Captain-lieutenant, and I am not proposing sending out a single corvette to hunt down a cruiser class vessel, especially not one as formidable as the Tau-zero-five. I am proposing sending out a task force comprised of the fastest capital ships currently docked at the station along with a couple of escort squadrons.'

'And you wish me to lead one of the escort squadrons? I think I see—'

'No *Captain* Strasky, you do not. I am promoting you to captain, first rank, and giving you command of the Admiral Kolulov, a Turovosk class cruiser – she's brand new. I want you to *command* the task force. Hunt down the Tau-zero-five, Captain, hunt it down and destroy it.'

'It will be done, Vice-admiral, you can count on me,' the newly promoted captain replied, saluting, his face beaming with pride.

***

The task force reached the outskirts of the Pegasus Nebula in a little over a week, Captain Strasky having ordered the Admiral Kululov's drives run at 105 per cent output for as long as his chief engineer dared. What remained of the

Aleksei Garin was soon located – a drifting hulk, wisps of plasma drifting from her crippled drives.

'Life signs?' Captain Strasky asked.

'None, Captain – I'm not detecting anything apart from trailing drive plasma,' a lieutenant replied, his voice hollow.

'I want a conference in my office, now,' Captain Strasky spat before storming from the bridge.

Three minutes later the captain was sitting in his office facing holograms of the captains of the three other capital ships in his task force.

'I take it you have all scanned the wreck?'

'Yes, Captain – we could not detect any life signs,' a heavily bearded captain replied.

'Perhaps they managed to launch lifeboats?' another of the assembled officers suggested.

'It does not look likely, Captain Gorev – we are picking up nothing on any of the emergency channels,' the third of the assembled captains responded.

'I concur with Captain Anyanev, the Aleksei Garin appears to have been lost with all hands,' Captain Strasky said, voicing the unspoken fear of all four officers.

'How do we proceed, Captain? The enemy is probably far from here by now.'

'That is a possibility, though I think it unlikely. The Tau-zero-five has so far eluded us: we have only even seen it once—'

'So what makes you think that it will still be *here*?' the bearded captain interrupted.

'Success, Captain Rytkin, often leads to over-confidence and a lack of caution. The Tau-zero-five is still here, Gentlemen – waiting to inflict a most humiliating blow on the Russian Federation.'

'She is waiting to attack the relief force that was sure to be sent,' Captain Anyanev said, a grim timbre in his voice.

'But if we haven't even—'

Beyond Earth: New Earth

'But nothing, Captain Rytkin, in second guessing the enemy we have robbed him of much of the surprise his cowardly tactics rely upon. We will search the nebular by grid cube. I will assign each of you a two-frigate escort – you will search the nebular whilst I will remain outside with the corvette squadron to coordinate.'

'With respect, Captain, but you haven't—'

'I haven't commanded a capital ship before. No, Captain Gorev, I have not. I am, however, the only person to have encountered the Tau-zero-five and survive. I am fully aware that you only command light cruisers and I am sending you each in effectively along – but it is the only way.' Captain Strasky answered his officer's unvoiced questions with a finality that would brook no disagreement.

For fifteen hours the light cruisers scoured the Pegasus Nebula in search of the Tau-zero-five. From the bridge of the Admiral Kululov, captain Strasky built up as complete a picture as he could of the search given the interference generated by the nebula.

'Lieutenant Rastyavik, what—' The captain was cut off mid-sentence as a colossal explosion tore through the ventral weapons array. 'STATUS!' the captain bellowed. Confusion reigned on the bridge for a couple of moments. 'I want to know what just happened!'

'Er, I—' a lieutenant began, at a loss for words.

'Simply and clearly, Lieutenant, what just happened?'

'An explosion in our forward ventral weapons array, Captain. Possibly a mine or a—'

'It wasn't a mine, Lieutenant,' the captain stated before turning to another of his bridge officers. 'Lieutenant Salyanov, have our scanners detected anything anomalous?'

'Actually, yes, Sir, they did. I'm having trouble interpreting it though.'

'You are trying to make sense of two signals that appear to be originating from our ventral weapons array, one blue-shifted towards us and the other red-shifted away from us, yes?'

'Yes, Captain. How did you—'

'Never mind how. Can you display the trajectory of the blue-shifted signal on the main view screen?'

'Yes, Captain, just a moment.'

'What is the status of the ventral array?' he asked as Lieutenant Salyanov made her calculations.

'Completely destroyed, Sir – most of the lower decks forward of the bridge have had to be sealed off,' another bridge officer reported just as Lieutenant Salyanov's plot appeared on the main view screen.

'Helmsman, roll us to bring our dorsal weapons to bear on Lieutenant Salyanov's plotted trajectory. Captain-lieutenant Tokorov, I want that trajectory mined with everything we've got. Dispatch the corvettes at once – we only have ten to fifteen minutes – and recall the task force, we have found the Tau-zero-five.'

'Aye, Sir,' the captain's second-in-command replied, his voice unsure.

The next eleven minutes passed in tense silence, Captain Strasky watching as the corvette squadron deployed deep space mines along the trajectory Lieutenant Salyanov had plotted.

'Captain, one of the corvettes is reporting sporadic contacts from within the nebula.'

'Tell them to return at once.' The captain's voice was calm, betraying little of the tension that he was feeling inside. His eyes fixed on the main view screen, the captain watched the corvette squadron deploy the last of their mines, come about, and return to the Admiral Kolulov at full speed.

Just as the escort vessels were leaving the minefield a pair of United Industries heavy destroyers flew out of the nebula, right along Lieutenant Salyanov's plotted trajectory. Multiple explosions lit up the void as the destroyers hit several mines. Half a minute later a cruiser appeared, followed by the Tau-zero-five itself. Both capital vessels immediately made severe course corrections in an attempt to avoid the minefield. The cruiser, a Stymphalian class vessel hit two mines before it could get clear. Captain Strasky watched in satisfaction as the starboard bow and beam were gutted by explosions. The Tau-zero-five had almost made it clear when its stern clipped a mine, crippling one of its main drives.

'Status of the enemy vessels, Lieutenant Salyanov?' the captain demanded.

'One of the destroyers is crippled, Captain – it appears to be attempting to disengage. The other one is less badly damaged and is on a course to intercept the corvettes. The cruiser appears to be turning about to bring its port weapons array to bear. The Tau-zero-five appears to be attempting to disengage, Sir.'

'That must not happen. Captain-lieutenant Tokorov, contact the corvettes, tell them I want them to prevent the Tau-zero-five from disengaging – at all costs,' Captain Strasky ordered.

'But what about that destroyer? Even outnumbered three-to-one, it still out-guns the corvettes.'

'The Tau-zero-five must *not* be allowed to escape, Captain-lieutenant. How long until we can target that destroyer?'

'Any minute now, Captain,' one of the bridge officers replied.

'Very well, open fire as soon as you can.'

As the Admiral Kolulov turned ponderously to bring her dorsal rail cannons to bear on the lone destroyer, the corvettes were already accelerating after the Tau-zero-five. As soon as the dorsal turrets could lock onto the U.I. escort, the cruiser's dorsal dispersion field dropped and the powerful weapons opened fire. Despite the velocity of the rail cannons' projectiles, it still took several seconds for them to reach their target. When they impacted a brief blue flash told of the dispersion field protecting the destroyer's starboard beam overloading and failing. A fraction of a second later a ripple of explosions split the vessel in two.

'Brace for impact!' Seconds later the bridge of the Admiral Kolulov shook as its port-side was raked by weapons fire.

'Report!' Captain-lieutenant Tokorov bellowed.

'Ion accelerator fire from the cruiser, Sir. Our fields held but they're currently operating on reserve capacitors – it will take several minutes to bleed that much energy away.'

'We don't *have* several minutes, Lieutenant. Helmsman, bring as around, I want our dorsal array locked on to that cruiser NOW!' the captain snapped. Slowly the Admiral Kolulov came about and rolled to bring her formidable rain cannons to bear on the closing cruiser.

'Coming around, Captain. We should be in a—'

'Brace for impact!' Again the bridge shook, this time it was the dorsal fields that bore the brunt of the assault.

'Captain, I'm reading several capacitors blown, our dorsal field is failing – we can't take another hit there,' captain Strasky's second-in-command reported, as calmly as he could.

'Thank you, Captain-lieutenant. How long until we are in a position to—-' The captain was cut off mid-sentence as the cruiser suddenly exploded.

'What—'

'Captain Strasky, this is Captain Anyanev of the Smetlivyy, do you require any assistance?'

'Captain Anyanev, thank you, but no; your intervention was timely and much appreciated, however. We have taken some damage but are still fully operational.' The captain turned to his second-in-command who called up a tactical display of the immediate area, 'It looks like Captains Gorev and Rytkin have just engaged the Tau-zero-five, Captain Anyanev. Let's make sure they don't take all the glory!'

'Indeed. I am moving to intercept now.'

By the time the Admiral Kolulov and the Smetlivyy reached the Tau-zero-five all that was left was a drifting hulk.

'Lieutenant Salyanov, is there anything worth salvaging?' Captain-lieutenant Tokorov asked.

'No, Sir – I doubt it – I'm not detecting anything from the wreck.'

'Very well,' he said before turning to the captain. 'Congratulations, Captain – you have successfully hunted down and destroyed the single largest threat the Russian Federation has yet faced.'

'Thank you, Captain-lieutenant. I think we had better return to Nostrovka Station, though I'm not looking forward to trying to explain to the vice-admiral how I managed to get half of her new cruiser destroyed…'

'I shouldn't worry, Captain – open with the good news first, that usually works for me!'

Dr S. Fern

PICAROON

Void Dancer docked with Dublin having completed her latest 'supply run'. That's what they were calling them these days, supply runs. This time Captain Krämer and his crew had bushwhacked a Pan Asian Alliance registered freighter on its way back from an ore refinery in the asteroid belt to New Earth. Henry disembarked and headed straight to the manufacturing sector rather than the command deck. In the early days Dublin's captain and his command staff had run the entire city-ship. It rapidly became clear that this could not continue and it wasn't long before various parts of the ship began to govern themselves. The captain didn't even try to maintain control, but rather began trading with the various self-governing regions: he still controlled the bridge and therefore the city-ship's command and control systems.

After a journey of just over an hour Henry arrived at Dublin Ores: the city-ship's centre for trading in any and all mined ores.

'Ship?' a clerk asked as Henry walked up to a vacant counter.

'Void Dancer.'

'Name?'

'Captain Henry Krämer.'

'Okay, Captain, what'll it be? Selling?'

'Yea, I've got some magnesium, some tin, some copper and a little palladium,' Henry replied, handing four sample containers over to the clerk.

'Palladium,' the clerk began, reading the label on the sample container, 'where did you get five tons of palladium from, Captain?' Henry raised both eyebrows in response. 'Say no more; I don't want to know, and if the sample analysis comes back okay, I don't much care. Take a seat, I'll have the results within an hour.'

Henry had only been waiting twenty minutes when the clerk called him back to the desk. Clearly having such valuable cargo had its advantages as well as its risks.

'Well, Captain, the analysis is clean. So long as the rest of it's as pure you'll have earned a pretty penny by the end of the day. Where're you docked?'

'Bay three, dock seven.'

'Okay, have the ores dockside by zero-three hundred tomorrow. Do you want to see the quote now?'

'Too right, Mate.'

The clerk passed a tablet across the counter. Henry skimmed down to the bottom of the displayed document. 'Fuckin' 'ell, we *did* get lucky. Thanks, Mate.' Henry passed the tablet back to the clerk and left the trade counter.

On his way back to the ship he picked up a couple of crates of beer and a bottle of starblood; with what the cargo would sell for they could afford to celebrate, and besides, they deserved a chance to unwind a bit. It was rarely possible to secure quarters when they were in port due to the extreme over-crowding across the city-ship. Henry had lost count of how long it had been since he had spent any significant amount of time off Void Dancer. He did what he could to ensure that everyone had at least some downtime and privacy aboard, but it wasn't always possible. Something had to be done, but what?

'What's the occasion, Cap?' Phoebe asked as Henry boarded the freighter.

'You won't believe how much this haul is going to get us, Phoebs.'

'Really?'

'Trust me. Here.' Henry tore open the top of one of the crates and tossed his chief engineer a can of beer.

'Thanks, Cap,' she replied, thrusting the can into one of the pockets of her coverall. Henry toured the ship, distributing beers as he did. By half past three the following morning Commander Hasanov had overseen the unloading and sale of the ores. As he entered the bridge he was greeted with a riotous applause.

'We've been paid?' Henry asked, slurring.

'We've been paid, Cap.' Another round of cheers.

'Great, then we can afford to open this!' Josh said, reaching for the bottle of starblood, kicking over a crate of empty beer cans in the process. Most of Void Dancer's officers were there, and they were drunk: many more crates had been added to the two Henry had initially provided.

The following day Void Dancer put to space. As the freighter sailed away from the city-ship the new structures that were being built out from it were clear to see: Dublin was being expanded. These extensions spread not only across the surface of the asteroid, but deep into it as well. Francesca noticed Henry staring intently at Dublin via one of the view screens and asked, 'Everything alright, Cap?'

'Er, yea, Fran'; everything's fine. I'm just thinking, that's all.'

'Okay. What course do you want us to take?'

'Take us towards the New Jupiter lanes.'

'Not the Asian refinery again?'

'No, we can't hit the same place twice in a row; it's too risky.'

'Righto, Cap.'

***

For the next week Void Dancer slipped between asteroids on her way towards the main shipping lanes that ran from New Jupiter to New Earth.

Henry was mid-way through breakfast when all the lights went out in the galley. 'Bollocks,' he said as the dull green emergency lights came on. After making his way slowly to the comm-link on the far wall he called up the bridge. 'Josh, why've we switched to silent running?'

'We've spotted a bulk carrier, Cap.'

'This far out?'

'Yea.'

'I'll be right up.' With a breakfast bar in one hand and a mug of coffee in the other Henry jogged out of the galley.

'Let's see it, Josh,' Henry said as he entered the bridge which was illuminated solely by dull green emergency lights and console glare.

'It's up there, on the main screen,' Josh replied.

Sure enough, picking its way through the asteroid belt was a Carter Resources bulk carrier.

'It must be a new captain,' Henry commented.

'Yea, that'd be my guess. I'd wager he was trying to take a short cut and got lost.'

'Yea, probably,' Henry replied before turning to address Lieutenant Martin who was on duty at the tactical station. 'Will', prepare to charge the lasers.'

'Aye, Cap … all three batteries ready to charge on your order.'

'Josh put us across her bow and open a channel.' A couple of seconds later Void Dancer's systems came back up to full power and the freighter shot out from behind the asteroid that had been concealing her from the Carter Resources vessel.

'Carter Resources vessel, this is Captain Henry Krämer of the Void Dancer. Heave to and prepare to be boarded.' The cumbersome ship began to turn. 'Will, charge the lasers and put a shot across her bow.'

'Across, Cap?'

'Yes, *across*, not *into*.'

'Aye, Cap.' A salvo from the forward turret was enough to convince the carrier's captain to do as he had been bidden.

'This is Captain Morano of the Carter Resources vessel Stellar Queen. Why have you stopped me?'

'I've stopped you, Captain Morano, because I want what's in your hold.'

'What do you mean you *want what's in my hold*? My hold's empty – except for a couple of broken mining rigs—'

'Which doubtless can be repaired and sold for a fine price, Captain. Now I've asked you once; I won't ask you again, prepare to be boarded.'

'You can't do this! And I'm sure you won't open fire: if you really want my cargo you won't risk destroying my ship.' Captain Morano's voice oozed over-confidence.

'Oh won't I? My tactical officer is a very good shot, Captain. From this distance he can shoot out your bridge and cripple your drives if I give the order…'

'Alright, I'll do what you want: a couple of rigs aren't worth dying over.'

'Josh, take us over there and dock with her. Will prepare a boarding party; I want to take the ship undamaged and with as few casualties as possible.'

'Aye Cap,' the lieutenant replied, a little bemused.

'Don't worry, Will, I'm not going soft: I've got an idea is all,' Henry replied as he rose from his chair.

'You're coming with us, Cap?' the lieutenant asked.

'Yea; as I said, I've got an idea,' Henry replied, smiling.

The captain, Lieutenant Martin and the boarding party were greeted by Captain Morano and fifteen very nervous looking crewmen. The captain was an obese man in his mid-forties with thin blonde hair and an unhealthy complexion. 'I'm Captain Morano,' he began, 'you're wasting your time: there's nothing on board, we're empty, well, mostly empty, there's just a few broken rigs aboard, that's all…'

'You're lying, Captain. Try again,' Henry said, drawing a pistol from his belt.

'Honestly, it's true—' Henry shot him mid-sentence and he hit the deck with a heavy thud.

'Now, let's try again shall we?' The remaining men shifted from one foot to the other for a second or two before one of them stepped forward; a tall, athletic man with a nose that had been broken too many times and a long scar that ran the length of his face.

'I'm the first mate. The name's Marco.'

'What're you carrying, Marco?' Henry asked.

'It's true, we do have several broken rigs aboard, but we're also carrying some refined ores: iron and nickel mostly, but there's also some cadmium and a little mercury.'

Henry turned from the first mate to address the other men who were standing behind him. 'See how I've not shot him? That's because he wasn't a dickhead. Now, I'm going to take this ship as well as its cargo. You've got a shuttle aboard, right?'

'Yes…' Marco replied with venom.

'Right. Then I'm going to make you an offer. You can either get on that shuttle and fuck off back to the refinery, or you can stay on board and work for me.' There were a variety of responses to Henry's offer from outright shock, to surprise, and apprehension. It was the look on Marco's face that held Henry's attention, however.

'What exactly are you offering us, Captain?' he asked, this time, with no hint of venom.

'Exactly the same as anyone else who works for me: a fair share of all our takings. I'd wager it's more than you're earning shipping rock, right?'

'I'm willing to take that chance. Alright, Captain, I'm in.'

'And the rest of you?' Henry asked. Ten agreed to stay while four refused and were escorted to Stellar Queen's shuttle. 'Right then, follow Void Dancer,' he said, once the bulk carrier's shuttle had departed.

'Oh, and one more thing,' he added as he turned to leave, 'You're on my crew now, so you're family, but if you betray me I'll fuck you up.' The crew of Stellar Queen looked at each other, unsure what they should do or say. Marco simply smiled. *'I'll have to watch that son of a bitch,'* he thought as he returned to Void Dancer.

After three hours of picking their way through asteroids a bright flash illuminated Stellar Queen's stern. The huge carrier began drifting away from Void Dancer.

'Void Dancer to Stellar Queen. Marco, what's going on over there?' Sylvia asked from the captain's chair.

Several seconds later Marco's voice crackled across the bridge. This is Stellar Queen. We've suffered a major accident – our main drive just blew. We're on emergency power and trying to correct our course drift with thrusters.'

'Understood, Stellar Queen. We'll come about. What can we do?'

'Nothing at the moment: We're still trying to figure out what happened.'

'Roger that Stellar Queen; we'll stand by,' she replied before cutting the link and raising the captain.

Several minutes later Henry walked onto the bridge in his old dressing gown and slippers. 'What's going on, Sylv?'

Void Dancer's second mate ran a hand through her spiky pink hair. 'It's not good Cap,' she sighed. 'Stellar Queen's suffered a catastrophic drive failure. They've only got thrusters now.'

'Let's have a look.'

Sylvia called up a view of the crippled carrier on the bridge's main view screen. She was moving painfully slowly around a spinning asteroid, her stern section blackened and torn.

'Who's on duty over there?'

'Marco. Do you want me to raise them?'

'Yea.'

'Stellar Queen, this is Void Dancer. Marco, come back. Over.'

'Sylvia, this is Marco. We can't get any more speed out of the thrusters: they're operating way above their rated maximums as it is.'

'Marco, this is Henry. What happened?'

'Our main drive failed a few minutes ago, Captain. We're having to manoeuvre with thrusters only now.'

'What do you mean *it failed*?'

'We thought it was an accident at first…'

'But now?'

'You better get over here, Captain.'

'Don't fuckin' move, Mate.' Henry yanked the pistol free from the holster that was strapped to the side of the captain's chair and stormed off the bridge.

'You two, go with him,' Sylvia said to two of the three on-duty bridge hands. The two men scampered off the bridge after their captain. They reached the freighter's shuttle bay just as Henry was boarding the shuttle.

'What're you two doing here?' he asked.

'Sylvia sent us,' one replied.

'Fair enough.' Sylvia had only just de-pressurised the shuttle bay and opened the doors when Henry gunned the engine and shot out into the void. He was greeted at Stellar Queen's starboard docking ring by Marco. The bulk carrier's first mate was flushed. There was blood running down the left side of his face.

'What the fuck's happened here?' Henry thought.

'Follow me.' Marco led Henry and the two bridge hands up to the carrier's galley. The room was a mess of upturned tables and chairs. In the centre of the room a man sat slumped in a chair, bound hand and foot. From the look of him he'd taken a severe beating.

'Who the fuck's this?' Henry asked.

'Antonio, the chief engineer.'

'He's responsible?'

'Yea; we detected a failure in the drive's coolant system shortly before it blew.'

'Shouldn't it have shut itself down automatically?'

'It should have, but it didn't.'

'You're sure it was him?'

'No one else could have isolated and shut down the fail-safes. There're two assistant engineers aboard, but they don't have the expertise.'

'Twat...can he still talk?'

'Probably not.'

'Fuck it. Void him.'

Marco didn't even pause, he just walked over to Antonio, cut his bonds with a galley knife, slung him over his shoulder and left the room. A few minutes later Marco opened the port docking ring and dropped Antonio into the airlock.

'I warned you,' Henry said as the battered man slowly pushed himself to his knees. He tried to say something but a swollen mouth full of broken teeth and blood prevented him. 'I don't give a shit, Mate; you betrayed me and now you're going to pay the price.' Henry didn't take his eyes from the engineer as he closed the door that led into the airlock. It slowly dawned on the chief engineer what was happening and he reached up to the window, a pleading look on his face. Henry opened the external door and Antonio was sucked out into the void.

'What'd we do now?' Marco asked.

'We find a suitable place to hole up,' Henry replied, turning from the airlock.

'Until we can find another drive? That won't be easy.'

'Yes and no. Yes we need to find another drive, but no; I'm looking for a permanent location.' Marco's brow furrowed. 'Trust me,' Henry said before turning and making his way back to Void Dancer's shuttle.

For the next day and a half Void Dancer, with Astral Queen following far in her wake, searched amongst the asteroids for a suitable place to conceal the bulk carrier.

Eventually a suitable location was discovered: a deep cavern in a particularly large asteroid.

'Can you get her inside?' Francesca asked over the comm-link.

'I think so. We're down to two thrusters, so I'll have to take her in port-first, but I think I can do it,' Marco replied. For the next hour the bulk carrier inched herself into the cavern.

'Void Dancer, this is Astral Queen, we're in and settled on the cavern floo – bollocks!'

'Marco – everything alright?'

Yea; it's okay. The last thruster just burned itself out, that's all. I hope Henry knows what he's doing; I doubt you'll ever get her out of here now.'

***

Once Stellar Queen's crew had been transferred to Void Dancer the bulk carrier was powered down and the freighter returned to Dublin. As soon as they docked Henry disembarked and went in search of Charles. After a couple of hours he finally found his friend with several others of Christina's crew in a dank seedy bar.

'Mate! How are you?' Henry asked.

'Alright, Mate? You staying long?' Charles replied.

'Of course!' he replied, taking a long draught of beer. 'Mind if I join you?'

'Feel free,' a woman replied gesturing, with an arm covered in post-burn scars, to an empty stool.

'Thanks; I'm Henry—'

'Henry Krämer, captain of the Void Dancer. I've heard about you.'

'Oh, really? And who might you be, Darling?' Henry replied, raising an eyebrow.

'Isabelle Ludnikov, captain of the Christine. Rumour has it you have a knack for *acquiring* valuable cargo?'

'I've been…lucky, lately.'

'More than lucky, if what we've heard is true,' someone added.

'A bit more than just lucky, if I'm honest. Look, I came here to talk to Charles…'

'It's alright, Mate; you can trust these guys.'

Henry looked around the table and then leaned in. 'I'm looking for a drive.'

'What kind of drive?' Charles asked. 'And why come to me?'

'I need a drive for a bulk carrier, Mate, but I need it on the quiet.'

'Why?' Isabelle asked.'

Henry was silent for a minute or two. After taking another draught of beer he lowered his voice further. 'I'm working on something. That *luck* you mentioned, what would you say if I said I'd be willing to cut you in on a little?'

'I'd say, keep talking,' Isabelle replied, emptying her beer into Henry's mug and passing her now empty one to another of her crew who then left the table.

'Well, you know how we rely on Dublin for everything?' A murmur of agreement answered his rhetorical question. 'Well imagine if that wasn't the case.'

'You thinking of leaving Dublin, Mate?' Charles asked.

'Not entirely, I'm thinking of setting up my own place.'

'Somewhere where we can set our own prices, you mean?' a short woman to Charles' left asked.

'That, and more. We'd be free to do what we want when we wanted. You want some downtime off-ship? You got it.'

'It sounds great, Fella', but you're just yankin' our chain, right?' a burly man next to Isabelle asked.

'No, Mate, I'm not. I've got a bulk carrier hidden away on an asteroid right now. It'd serve well enough as a start.'

'How? On second thoughts, I don't want to know,' Isabelle said.

'When you said *starting point* what did you mean?' the burly man asked.

'I've also got a couple of mining rigs that can be used to burrow into the asteroid. They need a bit of work but once they're up and running we'll be able to dig down and set up a real decent base.'

'So they're not working at the moment?' Charles asked.

'Not so much, but they just need a bit of work, trust me. Now, are you in or out?' he asked Isabelle.

'What's the catch? It sounds too good to be true.'

'Right, well, as I said, I need a drive for the carrier.'

'And?'

'And…' Henry thought for a moment, 'there'll be fees, but you can pay 'em with ammunition, fuel, food stores – stuff like that. We'll sort out the details later, Darlin'. What I need to know now is, are you in?' Henry gave her a wicked smile.

'What'd you think, Charles? You know this guy, can I trust him?'

'Henry? He's scum—'

'Thanks a fuckin'—'

'But you can trust him!'

'Alright, Captain Krämer, I'll accept your offer. I can get you your drive; give me a few days. I want to see what you've got before I commit to anything firm though, understand?'

'Fair's fair, Darlin'. As soon as you get the drive let me know and I'll show you what I've got.' Henry winked. A grin threatened to cross Isabelle's face.

'Well I think that calls for another round!' Charles said. 'Where's Rich'?'

'Here,' a short, bearded man replied as he placed a heavily laden tray on the table. 'Sorry, I got held up at the bar.'

Over the course of the next few hours Henry explained exactly what he had planned, or at least, that's what he told Isabelle and her crew. In actual fact he invented the majority of what he said, but no one seemed to notice. One by one the Christina's crew left the bar for their bunks, some more steadily than others. Henry was talking to Charles when Isabelle got up, rested her hand on his shoulder and gave him a look that left him in no doubt that he'd had his last beer that evening.

'See you later, Mate,' Charles said as he too downed his drink and got up to leave.

***

The following day Christine formed up alongside Void Dancer and the two ships headed out into the asteroids. Life was cramped aboard Void Dancer; the crew of Astral Queen were forced to re-arrange their temporary accommodation around the additional supplies the freighter had taken on overnight. They found Astral Queen just as they had left her: cold and lifeless. As Josh was bringing Void Dancer alongside the carrier's starboard docking ring Henry went to fetch his chief engineer.

'Phoebe, it's Henry; we've reached Astral Queen. Get your shit together and meet me at the starboard airlock,' he said, speaking into the intercom mounted next to the door to Phoebe's bunk.

Silence.

'Phoebe, you in there?'

Silence.

'I should have known,' he muttered as he walked off. A minute later he reached another set of quarters.

'Claire, you in there?' he asked the intercom.

'Yes Cap,' she replied. 'What's up?'

'Is Phoebe with you?'

'Just a sec.'

'What's up, Cap?' Phoebe asked a few seconds later.

'We've reached Astral Queen. I need you at the starboard airlock as soon as possible.'

'I'll be right out.'

As Phoebe stepped out of Claire's quarters a *clung!* reverberated through the ship.

'That Christine docking?' Phoebe asked as she pulled on a faded vest top and zipped up a pair of tattered trousers.

'Yea, Isabelle and a couple of others are coming over to check her out.'

'So it's *Isabelle* now, is it?' Phoebe asked with a sly grin as they made their way to the starboard airlock.

'That's her name…'

'I bet it's *Captain* to me though, right?'

'I don't know; you'll have to ask her.'

'Did you?'

'Once or twice…'

'You dog!' she laughed as they reached the starboard airlock. 'Has anyone been across yet?'

'No. We'll need the suits,' Henry replied as he opened one of the void suit lockers adjacent to the airlock.

They had just finished suiting up when Isabelle and the burly man that he had met in the bar at Dublin arrived.

'Alright, Isabelle and… '

'Dan, chief engineer,' the burly man replied.

'That's it. Sorry: it was a heavy night.'

's'ok.'

'This is Phoebe, my chief engineer.'

'Hi.'

'Please to meet you. May I presume that this carrier of yours isn't currently capable of supporting life, Henry?' Isabelle asked with more than a hint of doubt.

'We had to shut down the emergency power when we left. We'll only need suits until we turn it back on. They're in those lockers over there,' Henry said.

'Alright, fair enough,' Isabelle replied as she pulled a void suit out of one of the lockers.

As soon as Isabelle and her engineer had suited up they boarded Astral Queen and headed straight for the bridge and returned power to the carrier. Immediately power was restored void alarms began sounding on the bridge.

'It's just the engine room, Captain, it's nothing to worry about,' Phoebe replied.

'Nothing to worry about? I thought it was just a drive you needed, Henry?' Isabelle asked.

'It is, basically…'

'Put it this way,' Phoebe said, interrupting her captain. 'You'd have needed to remove a lot of the stern hull plating to get the replacement drive into the engine room anyway, right?'

'Fair point,' Dan replied.

'Let's take a look, shall we?' Isabelle said, leaving the bridge.

The engine room had suffered significant damage when the main drive failed. A large area to port was open to space where the hull plating had failed during the explosion.

'Well it's a mess, Henry,' Isabelle said over her suit's comm-link.

'It's repairable, though,' Dan put in.

'We didn't bring any spare hull plating, Dan. We could install the drive, sure, but—'

'S'alright, we picked a load of plating up back at Dublin,' Henry interrupted.

'You're full of surprises, Henry, I'll give you that. Okay, I've seen enough. Dan?'

'Yea, Captain: this is doable.'

'In which case, you've got your drive, Henry. Don't let me down.'

'I won't, trust me.'

'Er, Cap, can we head back via the aft hold? I'd like to get Dan's opinion on those rigs,' Phoebe asked as they turned to leave.

'Yea; sounds like a good idea.'

The three mining rigs were huge, but even they were dwarfed by the enormity of the aft cargo hold. After looking them over, the two engineers discovered that it was the gearboxes that had failed.

'We've got some ideas,' Phoebe began, once they had finished their inspection.

'Go on,' Isabelle said.

'Well, it looks like the gearboxes need replacing. They're jobs that couldn't be done on site, which is why they were being shipped back to New Earth.'

'I hope you're about to say you can fix 'em,' Henry said.

'We think so, Cap,' Phoebe answered. 'We'll have to be inventive, but we think we can do it. We'll need some parts but Dan says he knows a few places in Dublin, what with his having sourced Christine's new drive and all.'

'Alright, sounds good to me,' Henry replied. 'Isabelle?'

'It sounds okay to me.'

'Well the sooner we get started, the sooner we can get back to normal on the Dancer,' Phoebe said.

'Yea, and not a minute too soon either,' Henry added.

***

Astral Queen's repairs took a full month to complete, but it was a further couple of weeks before the two chief engineers were happy enough with them to allow Henry to begin transferring her crew back aboard. Once the repairs to the carrier were finished Christine departed and returned to Dublin to retrieve the parts that would be required to recommission the three mining rigs. During this time Henry planned out the first phase of the expansion he had in mind. He wanted store houses, fuel dumps and ammunition lockers bored out of the asteroid. He gave over all command of the base, which retained the name Astral Queen, to Francesca, promoted Sylvia to first mate, Josh to second, and took on Marco as his third. Phoebe spent the couple of weeks that Christina was away teaching Astral Queen's assistant engineers everything they would need to keep the bulk carrier running now that they didn't have a chief engineer of their own. Once Christina returned with the spare parts, Phoebe, Dan and as many of the freighters' assistant engineers as were available were tasked with repairing the huge machines and working out how to operate them. Fortunately they were almost entirely automated and only required a few crew each.

Once she had delivered the spare parts and they were up and running, Isabelle took Christine back out into the asteroid belt on a *supply run*, leaving Phoebe to train the carrier's crew in the operation of the rigs. Void Dancer; therefore, wasn't able to put to space for another few months. Henry wasn't too bothered by this: he'd ensured they had taken on plenty of supplies before they left Dublin.

***

'Well, that's it, Commander; all three rigs are up and running,' Phoebe said as she entered Astral Queen's bridge.

'Commander?' Henry asked.

'Yes, Cap, I thought that since I'm in charge around here I deserved a rank of some kind. Astral Queen's not really a ship anymore, so *captain* didn't seem appropriate, but *commander*, now that had a ring to it that I liked!' Francesca said.

'Fair enough, *Commander*! So you're happy with things as they are?'

'Yes, thanks, Cap: Phoebe's done a great job. I think we'll be fine here now; just don't forget to keep the supplies coming in!'

'Yea, we'll begin to stockpile over the next few months. You'll be running a fully fledged space station before you know it!'

'I do hope so!'

'I'm planning on taking Void Dancer out in the next few hours. Besides the obvious, is there anything you want us to pick up while we're away?'

'How about a small freighter or carrier or something like that?'

'You're serious? What could you possibly want with another ship for? You're not thinking of building a fleet of your own are you, Fran?'

'No, Cap; I've a feeling running this place will keep me busy enough. I've been thinking about the future. At the moment we can only have a single ship docked at a time. I know you'd planned to extend the dorsal superstructure and construct a docking bay, but that'd be a huge project and I'm not sure we've got the resources, not to mention the manpower, for such a project at the moment, but I've had an idea. You see, if you could *acquire* a second vessel, all we'd need to do is mount it dorsally and bang! We'd have another two docking points – assuming the ship in question had a port and starboard airlock.'

'Sorry, Fran, are you suggesting we just *weld* one ship to another?' Phoebe was incredulous.

'Basically, yes. There'd be a bit of internal work to do, but it'd be a lot easier than building a whole load of extra superstructure from scratch, right?'

Phoebe began to laugh.

'She clearly thinks you're as mad as I do! Come off it, Fran,' Henry said.

'No!' Phoebe said between bouts of laughter, 'Well, yes! Fran, you're mad! The crazy thing is, in principle, it's by far the easiest way to increase Astral Queen's capacity. It's just a ridiculous idea: attaching ships together like they're children's building bricks!'

'So you think it's doable?' Francesca asked, smiling.

'Yes, Fran, I think it's doable, so long as the cap can get you a suitable ship without blowing the shit out of it!'

'Hey! I'm not a fuckin' psychopath… I just don't like it when people start taking the piss!'

'No, of course not, Cap! You—'

'Commander? I've got an incoming message from Christine,' one of the bridge hands said.

'Okay, put it through, Steve,' Francesca replied.

'Astral Queen, this is Christine requesting permission to dock.'

'How long before Void Dancer's ready to leave, Cap?' Francesca asked.

'She's ready now, to be honest. Are you trying to get rid of me, *Commander*?!'

'No, of course not, it's just that we've only got capacity to accept a single vessel at the moment. She'll have to piggyback on to Void Dancer if she comes in now and then you'll be stuck here until she leaves.'

'I'm just messin' with you, Fran – I'll be out of your hair in half an hour. Come on Phoebs, the commander has a space station to run!'

'See you soon, Fran – good luck!'

'Thanks, Phoebe. Take care you two, and don't forget to bring me back another ship!'

'We won't!' Henry said as he left the bridge.

Half an hour later Void Dancer was heading back out into the asteroid belt as Christine, with a full hold, was docking with Astral Queen.

***

'Where to, Captain?' Marco asked once Void Dancer had cleared Astral Queen.

'Towards the New Jupiter lanes, Mate; I feel like picking a fight with someone,' Henry replied, opening a can of beer.

'No problem, Captain,' Marco replied.

'You're not still pissed about the Astral Queen are you?' Henry asked.

'Me? No. Do I sound it?'

'Well you haven't smiled once since we met.'

'I wouldn't worry about it, Captain; most people think I'm a miserable son of a bitch most of the time. The truth is I don't tend to smile unless there's something to smile about, and shipping ore from one end of the system to the other is hardly a barrel of laughs.'

'Well, cheer up, Mate; you're not shipping rocks now! Beer?'

'Thanks.' Void Dancer's third mate caught the can Henry tossed almost without looking.

'So you've got yourself a space station now, Captain; what do you plan to do?'

'Seriously? Get rich, Mate.'

'I can live with that,' Marco said as a smile crossed his face for the first time in years. He took a swig of beer, made a slight course alteration, and sat back as Void Dancer slipped between the asteroids on her way to the rich hunting grounds of the New Jupiter shipping lanes.

Beyond Earth: New Earth

RETURN TO THE ANDERSON SYSTEM

The bulk carrier U5475 orbited Liberty One. Officially mothballed several years ago, the huge vessel drew no attention from anyone; she was just another old ship that appeared to have avoided scrapping – always someone else's responsibility. Equally unnoticed was the shuttle that departed the space station and made the short journey to the derelict vessel.

'Hard seal acquired. You're clear to disembark, Doctor,' the shuttle pilot said, half turning to his only passenger.

'Thank you, Pilot,' Doctor Silvia Cranbrook said. United Industries' head of biomedical science disembarked the shuttle and stepped into a well-lit security office that was entirely at odds with the carrier's dilapidated exterior.

'Doctor Silvia Cranbrook,' she said, without waiting for the security officer to ask. She put her third finger into a small orifice in the officer's desk. After receiving a small sharp scratch she withdrew her finger and waited. A minute or two later the words 'D.N.A. check complete. Identification verified' were illuminated in green and the officer unlocked the door that led into the next room. The next room was bare except for a terminal mounted on the far wall next to the room's only other door. Doctor Cranbrook walked up to the terminal, placed her eye against a small lens and punched the 'Verify' button. A few seconds later the door adjacent to the retinal scanner unlocked and she entered the ship proper.

'Doctor Cranbrook, good morning. You are expected in meeting room three,' the receptionist said from behind a large desk.

'Good. Everyone is present?'

'Yes, Doctor; Doctor Fairborne arrived a few minutes ago.'

'I suppose it's a miracle he arrived at all,' she thought as she walked down the corridor, past numerous laboratories and made her way to meeting room three.

It was a small gathering: Doctor Milsen, the company technical director; Doctor Fairborne, the head of advanced technologies and high energy physics, and three other scientists were present. Doctor Milsen was, as ever, immaculately dressed and surrounded by a thick haze of cigarette smoke. Doctor Fairborne was instantly recognisable. He stood out from his fellow scientists thanks to his scruffy clothes, untidy shoulder-length hair and straggly goatee.

'Aah, Doctor Cranbrook, welcome – good morning!' Doctor Fairborne said, stepping over, taking Doctor Cranbrook's hand and shaking it vigorously.

'Doctor Fairborne, you have recovered, I see,' she replied.

Taking back his hand, the doctor ran a hand over his horribly scarred face and bionic eye. 'Ah, yes… well… I'm up and running, so to speak.'

'Which is more than I can say for dock six,' Doctor Milsen put in acidly.

'It's still out of operation?' Doctor Cranbrook asked. Liberty One's sixth dock had been completely destroyed when a prototype space mine, based on the information retrieved from the Russian Federation Admiralty archives, exploded prematurely.

'I suppose this is one of the few occasions when we can be thankful that the prototype didn't perform as expected!' Doctor Fairborne laughed.

Beyond Earth: New Earth

'The loss of an entire dock is no laughing matter, Doctor. It's a very good thing that I have the ear of the chairman or we could have seen our work under much closer scrutiny,' Doctor Milsen snapped, lighting another cigarette. 'Now, I suggest we turn to the matter at hand. Doctor Cranbrook, if you could begin the proceedings I would be grateful.'

'Certainly,' she began. 'Some years ago we recovered the survey vessel Forscher, on lease to Huber Bergbau. She was transmitting an S.O.S. and had been drifting for several days when we found her. We removed from her side what we thought to be an asteroid. We were wrong; it was some sort of alien—'

'Were there any survivors?' one of the three other scientists asked.

'No, the creature killed everyone on board and had begun to consume various parts of the ship by the time we arrived.'

'It was fortunate that you were in the region, Doctor, or we might never have recovered the specimen,' another of the scientists put in.

'Yes, we were very fortunate. Anyway, as I was about to say, we recovered the specimen and managed to subdue it with a mixture of gasses. A couple of years later a Pan Asian Alliance settlement in the Anderson System met with a similar fate to the Forscher. We monitored the ill-fated rescue mission that was dispatched and gathered valuable information from it which served to further our research greatly.'

'Which is where my work comes in, I believe,' Doctor Fairborne said as he flicked between numerous tablets.

'There is one further point that should be reiterated,' Doctor Milsen interjected. 'The 'Asian Alliance aren't the only ones to have suffered incidents in the Anderson System; they were merely the first. Every major venture in the system has come to grief, more than once. This has led to every investor pulling their resources out of the system.

As a result Epsilon Gate has been running at a significant loss for three years now.'

'I'm sorry, Doctor, but can I assume from what you just said that the Anderson System gateway station is still operational and hasn't yet been attacked?' The first scientist asked.

'That is correct, Doctor Clements. We don't know why, but it doesn't do to question one's fortune. Suffice to say I am hoping that today's demonstration will prove a resounding success.' The technical director couldn't help but glance over to Doctor Fairborne as he made his last comment.

'Oh, it will be, it will be. We have conducted extensive tests already,' the scruffy doctor asserted.

'You have only a single specimen, correct?'

'Well, yes.'

'So how can you have conducted extensive tests, unless the vast majority of those tests were unsuccessful?'

'The creature has a remarkable capacity to regenerate, Doctor. After testing the creature is permitted sufficient nutrients to heal whatever damage it suffered. It has proven to be a most useful trait,' Doctor Cranbrook explained. The third scientist, that had as yet remained silent, appeared slightly nauseated as this last detail.

'I see. Well, I hope it was worth it?'

'Oh yes, Doctor. We had a couple of setbacks, but what project doesn't? Ha! Well, yes, so we have developed a weapon that has proven most effective against Doctor Cranbrook's specimen. Initially we came up with a number of possible—'

'Doctor, please!'

'Ah, yes, I'm sorry. Er, well, yes, we finally settled on what we've come to call the gamma lance. It's not a very—'

'Doctor Fairborne! I don't care what it's called! What *is* it?' Doctor Milsen took a long drag on his cigarette.

'Right, yes. It's basically an extremely high energy gamma ray beam. It operates in a similar way to a laser, just at a much higher energy – much higher...' a strange vacant look entered Doctor Fairborne's eyes as he trailed off.

'Please, allow me, Doctor,' Doctor Cranbrook began, taking over from her distracted colleague. 'The specimen we have has proven incredibly resilient to standard energy-based weapons: lasers, ion projectors, even rail guns. Doctor Clements, why don't you explain?'

'Certainly. All current weaponry works by destroying the outer shell of its target. Only then can significant damage be inflicted. This is true of people as well as vehicles etc. What we needed was a weapon that could penetrate *beyond* the specimen's impervious outer shell and damage its interior. The gamma lance does just that; the rays penetrate deep into the target, irradiating everything as they do so. This results in rapid cellular collapse. Our knowledge of the specimen's interior is still very vague, but the results are indisputable.'

'That's true, Doctor; the specimen has proven unable to regenerate tissues damaged by the gamma lance,' the third scientist added.

'Well this sounds very promising. I hope there is enough of the specimen remaining for a final demonstration?'

'Yes, Doctor, there is. Shall we?' Doctor Cranbrook asked as she rose from her seat.

'Certainly, lead on.' The technical director rose to his feet, pulled a cigarette from his frock coat and lit it as he left the room. The small party made their way through the converted bulk carrier to an observation gallery above one of the vessel's holds.

The creature in the hold was little more than a husk; its seed-like main body was withered, pock-marked and scored with deep wounds. Where before it had many tentacle-like arms, now it had only three, and even they showed signs of having been scorched and burnt.

'That's it?' Doctor Milsen asked, pressing his face to the glass.

'What's left of it, yes,' Doctor Fairborne replied. 'Shall we begin?'

'Certainly.'

'Claude; proceed at once – full power,' Doctor Fairborne said, turning to the third scientist.

'Full power, Doctor?'

'Yes – we won't need the specimen after this test.'

'Yes, Doctor.' Claude crossed the gallery to a control panel and began manipulating the controls. In the hold a large beam weapon that looked like an over-sized laser swung into position above the alien. 'I'm sorry,' Claude whispered as he set the weapon to full power and opened fire.

'Well go on then,' Doctor Milsen said.

'We have, Doctor. The ray is invisible to the human eye but the effects are not—'

'See there, Doctor,' Doctor Cranbrook interrupted as the alien began to spasm. 'The effects are not immediate but they are pronounced.' After a few moments convulsing in the hold the alien stopped moving and a sludge-like fluid began oozing from the mouths at the end of its three ravaged tentacles and black blotches began appearing on its grey outer shell.

'That is superb,' Doctor Milsen announced.

'It's certainly effective,' Doctor Cranbrook said.

'How long before we can begin production?'

'I have already spoken to department eighty-six. It will take them eight months to convert one of their production lines, or eighteen months to build a brand new one. After that, they expect to be able to turn out a weapon a week.'

'One a week, is that it? And what about ships to mount them? Have you thought about that, Doctor?'

'Yes. Due to the amount of power required to operate the lance they will not be able to be mounted anything smaller than cruiser class vessels. I would recommend laying down new ships as soon as possible, Doctor.'

Doctor Milsen let out a lungful of smoke, sighing as he did. 'This was never going to be a small project, was it? Still if what I've seen today is anything to go by we may very well be able to re-take the Anderson System and bring Epsilon Gate back to profitability.'

'Don't forget, Doctor, that if we retain this as proprietary technology our customers will need escorting whilst in-system,' Doctor Cranbrook added.

'Quite; I don't think this will be difficult to sell to the board. Thank you for the demonstration. Doctor Cranbrook, Doctor Fairborne, Doctors.' Doctor Milsen turned and left the gallery in a cloud of cigarette smoke.

The technical director was right: he did indeed have the chairman's ear. He convinced the board to agree to fund a new factory solely for the production of gamma lances. Further funding was provided for a new 'Anderson Fleet' armed primarily with the new weapons.

Two years later the new vessels were ready to put to space. The fleet was composed of five vessels: Uγ1, a heavy cruiser and Uγ2, 3, 4, and 5, which were all cruiser class vessels. As soon as the fleet was ready it was dispatched to Epsilon Gate with all haste – the Anderson System had to be brought back to profitability as soon as possible.

***

'Captain Farkas, this is Epsilon Gate; your fleet is cleared for transit.'

'Thank you, Epsion Gate,' Katalin Farkas, captain of the heavy cruiser Uγ1 replied from the captain's chair before cutting the link with the gateway station and leading her small fleet into the wormhole. Fifteen minutes later Captain Farkas' fleet was in the Anderson System. Her orders were to patrol the outer reaches of the system and engage and destroy any non-human vessels encountered.

'Captain Farkas, this is Anderson One, transit control; welcome to the Anderson System.'

'This is Captain Farkas of Uγ1, thank you, Anderson One.'

'Is there anything we can do to help, Captain?'

'Anderson One; no, I don't think so, thank you.'

'Understood, Captain... Good luck.' The tone of the transit controller's voice caused several of the bridge crew to share worried glances. They had all heard rumours of what may or may not have caused the Anderson System to be abandoned.

'That's enough, all of you; you're officers of the United Industries Navy, not superstitious civvies. Pull yourself together!' the captain barked. 'Mr Rodríguez, have the fleet adopt formation alpha.'

'Aye, Captain,' the helmsman replied.

In response to Captain Farkas' order cruisers Uγ2 and Uγ3 formed up into a wedge with Uγ1 at its apex. Uγ4 and Uγ5 took up positions above and below the main wedge. In this manner Captain Farkas' fleet began its patrol of the Anderson System's outer reaches.

***

A week and a half into their patrol Uγ1 received a priority transmission from Uγ4.

'Let's hear it,' Captain Farkas said.

'Uγ1, this is Uγ4 we have a strange reading on the long-range scanners.'

'Can you identify it, Captain Harris?'

'No, Captain, whatever it is it looks like it originated from the fifth planet, or one of its moons.'

'Acknowledged, Uγ4. Stand by.' Captain Farkas called up a plot of her fleet on one of the bridge's secondary view

Beyond Earth: New Earth

screens. 'Mr Rodríguez, plot a course to intercept Captain Harris' signal and send it out to the rest of the fleet.'

'Aye, Captain,' the helmsman replied.

As one, the fleet changed course and closed in on the unidentified contact. After several minutes it was detected by the rest of the fleet's long-range scanners. Half an hour later it was within range of the fleet's short-range scanners. After a further fifteen minutes it was visible on the main view screen. Over a period of a few minutes the contact resolved itself into three tear-drop shaped vessels that trailed tendrils. Delicate frills ran the length of the blue-green ships.

Captain Farkas activated her chair-mounted intercom, set it to broadcast fleet-wide and began giving orders. 'Uγ2 and Uγ4, engage the highlighted vessel,' she began as she highlighted one of the alien vessels on the view screen. 'Uγ3 and Uγ5, engage the highlighted vessel,' she continued as she highlighted a second alien. 'Lieutenant Scott, we will engage the third vessel, prepare all batteries for firing.'

'Aye, Captain,' the tactical officer replied.

As the range between the opposing vessels closed the Captain Farkas' cruisers broke formation and peeled off to engage their designated targets. Uγ1's heading remained unchanged and she sailed straight towards the third alien ship.

'Captain, shouldn't we change course? We can't target the enemy with our stern batteries if we remain on this heading,' Commander Marković, Uγ1's executive officer, asked.

'No, Commander, all the intelligence we have suggests that they're a lot more manoeuvrable than we are. If we changed course for a broadside we would put ourselves at considerable risk. If that *thing* manages to close with us we're dead.'

'But we're armed with *heavy* gamma lances, surely a single broadside should be sufficient?'

'It should be, Commander, but I'm not going to take any chances. Trust me.'

'Always, Captain.'

'Thank you, Commander. Mr Rodríguez, prepare for a course alteration. Lieutenant Scott, prepare to open fire.' The tension on the bridge grew as the two vessels closed with each other.

'We're within range, Captain,' Lieutenant Scott announced.

'Thank you, Lieutenant.'

'Our cruisers have now engaged the enemy, Captain,' the lieutenant announced, his tone strained.

'You will hold fire until the captain orders you to open fire, Lieutenant,' Commander Marković snapped.

'Aye, Sir. Sorry, Sir.'

'Mr Rodríguez...' the captain began, 'thirty degree down angle! Roll to starboard!' As the range between the two ships closed to within spitting distance the heavy cruiser slipped below the alien, its two dorsal and two ventral turrets training as she did.

'Lieutenant Scott, open fire!' There was a disconcerting lack of recoil, or indeed any indication on the main view screen that the heavy cruiser had fired at all, barring the bright flash of an energy field failing.

'Mr Rodríguez, thirty degrees up and hard to port: bring us across her stern! Lieutenant Scott fire again as soon as you're able!' The captain was leaning forward in her chair, straining her eyes for any indication that her opening salvo had inflicted any damage whatsoever. The alien ship began turning sharply, trying to come about. Mr Rodríguez managed to keep the heavy cruiser rolling across the alien's stern and was coming over its top when the heavy gamma lances fired again.

'Well done, Mr Rodríguez; try to keep us above it – I don't want to get anywhere near those tentacles. The alien was far more manoeuvrable than Uγ1 however. By the time the heavy cruiser's lance batteries were ready to fire again the ship was broadside to the alien's bow.

'Oh Hell… is there any indication that we've inflicted any damage whatsoever, Commander?' Captain Farkas asked, concern building in her voice as the alien closed with her ship.

'Erm…'the commander began as his fingers danced across his console. 'I'm not sure, Captain. I don't even know what I'm looking for…'

'Damn! Prepare to repel boarders!' she shouted as the alien ship filled the view screen.

'Wait, Captain, look!' Rodríguez shouted from the helm.

'What is it, Mr Rodríguez?'

'There, Captain, can you see? The tentacles on its underside, they're bleeding, or something… See, there!'

Captain and Commander alike strained their eyes.

'He's right, Captain. Lieutenant Scott, open fire with everything, now!' the commander ordered.

'But, Sir, the main batteries haven't re-armed yet.'

'I said *everything*, Lieutenant, now fire the secondary batteries NOW!'

'Aye, Sir.'

A few seconds later $U\gamma 1$'s ion cannon batteries opened fire on the rapidly closing alien vessel. The bow of the alien disintegrated under the weight of fire and a torrent of foul sludge-like material spilled into space.

'How? I didn't think…' Lieutenant Scott whispered as the alien ship's innards filled the view screen.

'I read the intelligence reports too, Captain. It was a bit of a guess, to be honest, but I suspected that the lances would affect the ship's outer hull as well as its insides,' Commander Marković said.

'It would appear that you were right, Commander. Perhaps the radiation degraded the outer hull to such a degree that it became brittle enough to be affected by conventional weapons.'

'Captain, our cruisers report all enemy vessels destroyed,' one of the bridge officers reported.

'Congratulations, Captain, you have defeated an heretofore invincible foe,' the commander announced.

Captain Farkas smiled as an applause rippled across the bridge. 'Let's go home; our mission is complete.'

***

The board meeting had been going on for some time and United Industries' technical director was getting to the end of his tether. 'I recognise that it was a short patrol, but its objective was not to liberate the whole of the Anderson System, General,' Doctor Milsen said, rebutting another of the chief operations officer's criticisms. 'The purpose of the patrol, as I have already said, was solely to ascertain that the newly developed lances were as effective in reality as the testing suggested that they would be: there's only so much a scale-up trial can show – at some point you have to test a product in the market.'

'That's another thing, Doctor, your report recommends that we do not release this technology to the market. Are you aware how profitable this product could be?' the sales director, a sinewy woman in her early fifties, asked.

'Yes, Lily, I am quite aware how profitable it could be. However, the gamma lance is so much more powerful than any other weapon we currently provide that whilst we might make a small fortune in the short run, we would suffer a crippling drop in sales of our other systems... not to mention the fact that we don't yet have an effective defence against the lance.'

'That's a good point: we can't afford to release a product onto the market that we can't counter,' General Moore put in.

'And then there's the moral issue. What you've developed, Doctor, is, when all is said and done, a terribly effective irradiation beam, and whilst it is fine for use against alien lifeforms, it cannot be used against humans. To do so would—'

'Oh, for goodness' sake, Frank, it's a weapon, just like any other,' the general interrupted Alex, the stocky finance director.

'I think that regardless of any misgivings we may have, what we have is a weapon system that we cannot release on the open market,' Mr Nielsen, the chairman, said, bringing the meeting back to topic. 'I am inclined to agree with Doctor Milsen; we have a great opportunity here to secure the Anderson System and in so doing turn a loss-making asset into one of our most profitable. I therefore support the doctor's proposal that the Anderson fleet be expanded and that we make the gamma lance available for lease *only*, on a limited number of platforms. We will, in this way, maximise the system's potential profitability whilst ensuring our customer's security only so long as they are willing to invest sufficiently in it. I would like to conclude this meeting by thanking Doctor Milsen and his team publicly for all the work they have done in enabling United Industries to return to the Anderson System. Ladies and gentlemen, that will be all. Thank you.'

Dr S. Fern

Beyond Earth: New Earth

Also by the same author

Dr S. Fern

Pandemonium Ascendant

A dark fantasy set in a world of swords and sorcery

Fleeing the Corsair Coast, the fugitive sorcerer Dakuran El-Alamir and his companion Mikhael travel west towards the Plains of Madness in search of power. Seeking to unite the might of the Abyss with that of Pandemonium, Dakuran would rule the whole of the known world. Standing in his way, however, is the kingdom of the Eittendorfer and the fastness of Castle Wundigstein.

Will the stone of Wundigstein and the mettle of those who defend it turn the chaotic tide that has been unleashed, or will the streets of this mighty fortress-city echo with the cries of daemons; a foretaste of the doom to come?

Beyond Earth: New Earth

Dr S. Fern

Lightning Source UK Ltd.
Milton Keynes UK
UKOW01f2338021116
286777UK00004B/155/P